APOLLO'S SEED

After five years apart, Martha had been virtually forced to return to Greece to live with her husband Dion. She soon realised that her feelings for Dion were as strong as ever—but what about him? Wasn't it only too clear that his only reason for wanting her was to get their child back? And could she be sure he wouldn't take her daughter away from her altogether?

APOLLO'S SEED

BY

ANNE MATHER

MILLS & BOON LIMITED
17–19 FOLEY STREET
LONDON W1A 1DR

First published 1979
Australian copyright 1979
Philippine copyright 1979
This edition 1979

© Anne Mather 1979

ISBN 0 263 73145 6

Set in Linotype Plantin 10 on 11 pt.

Made and printed in Great Britain by
Richard Clay (The Chaucer Press), Ltd., Bungay, Suffolk

CHAPTER ONE

It was the air she had forgotten, its softness and clarity, the translucent light that made the colours more vivid, and the contrasts more pronounced. Then there was the smell— a distinctive aroma of lemon groves and pomegranate trees, and vines, luscious with ripening fruit. There was nowhere quite like it, and although her love for the islands had been tempered by other emotions, Martha still found it impossible not to respond to their seductive appeal.

She had awakened very early that morning, a not unusual circumstance considering she had gone to bed before ten, she had told herself, ignoring completely the fact that she had not slept well. Not even the two glasses of *ouzo* she had swallowed, in an attempt to get a good night's rest, had succeeded in ridding her mind of the problems she faced in the morning, and the night had been spent in uneasy remembrance of a life she had left more than five years ago.

But it was morning now, and from the balcony of her hotel she had a magnificent view of the blue-green waters of the Aegean, with the shadowy coastline of Turkey only a dozen or more miles away. A haze hung on the horizon, a promise of heat to come, but already the air was pleasantly warm and audible with the persistent hum of the *cicadas*.

She had chosen this hotel because it was near enough to the small town of Rhodes to permit her to ride there in a taxi in less than ten minutes, and not as far along the coast road as the hotel where she and Sarah had stayed almost eight years ago. It would have been too painful, she acknowledged, to stay at the same hotel—primarily, she added

5

bitterly, because it reminded her so strongly of the youth she had wasted.

The swimming pool in the grounds of the hotel below her was already attracting several of the guests, and watching a pallid-skinned teenager do an energetic crawl across its depth, she glanced down at her own pale arms and legs, visible below the candy-stripe of her nightshirt. Wintering in northern climes was certainly a drain on any tan she had had left from the previous year's trip to the Scilly Isles, and she envied those dark-skinned people who never looked pale and anaemic. Like Dion, she thought, and then grimaced when she realised his name had come automatically to mind. But, considering why she was here, that was not so surprising, she told herself severely, as she left the balcony to bathe and dress.

Nevertheless, having breakfast in the hotel dining room, she felt rather less sure of herself. It wasn't the first time she had wished she had not allowed herself to be persuaded to come here, and she doubted it would be the last. She wanted to help Roger, of course she did, but this particular demand was surely too much to expect. There *must* be some other way he could tackle it. And yet wasn't that exactly why she was here? Because there was no other way? Because the Myconos family had already blocked every other overture he had made?

She sighed, spreading the contents of a tiny tin of apricot conserve across a rather rubbery roll. If only it had been anywhere else than Mycos. Almost any other island! But Roger's research had led him to believe that Mycos might have given refuge to the Minoans, fleeing the tidal wave that devastated Crete when the volcanic island of Santorini erupted almost three thousand years ago. And although Martha had not wanted to get involved, his persistent assertion that the reason she wouldn't help him was because she was *afraid* to contact Dion again had gradually eroded her opposition.

Aware of the dark eyes of a waiter resting upon her, she felt an unwelcome shiver of apprehension slide down her spine. Greek men could be so contemptuous of Western European women. Their eyes admired their slender long-legged beauty, they showered extravagant compliments upon them—but secretly they despised their freedom and independence, even while they were taking advantage of it. Their own women were treated much differently. A Greek girl was still a virgin when she got married, and although her position was in no way equal to that of her husband, she was given his loyalty and fidelity, and the respect due to the mother of his children.

Martha pushed her plate aside half impatiently, and reached for the coffee pot. What was she doing? she asked herself, thinking about such things. They were not her concern—not any longer, at any rate. She had had enough of that kind of confinement, the cloistered life that left a man free to do as he wished, and a woman to do as she was told. If so total a commitment was respect, she could do without it. It was sad for Josy, of course it was, but at least she would have the freedom to do as *she* liked, and not as her father willed.

The guilt that invariably accompanied this silent defiance spilled over her once again. In all these years, she had not learned the art of self-deception. No matter what she said, no matter how she defended herself, she could never entirely destroy the feeling that she had deliberately deprived the child of her birthright. It was easy enough to state the facts—that Dion hadn't wanted to listen to her, that he had jumped to reckless conclusions without any proof, that he had driven her away by his absurd jealousy—but there was no denying that she had not denied his belief, had actually enjoyed his almost homicidal fury, and felt a certain smug satisfaction in thwarting him at last.

Those feelings had not lasted long. Indeed, she knew that had he come looking for her in those early days, she would have capitulated and told him the truth. She had loved him, after all, in spite of his faults, and it was not her nature to inflict pain. But he had not, and her hopes had turned to anger, and her anger to resentment, and resentment into bitterness. By the time she did receive a communication from him, Sarah had had her accident, and it was too late then to listen to reason. She had wanted nothing from him. His willingness to condemn her was unforgivable, and later, as her daughter developed into an adorable little girl, she had realised that if Dion ever learned that Josy was his, he might well take her from them, as well as everything else ...

Leaving the table, she crossed the tiled floor to the arched exit which gave access to the verandah. It was too early yet to take the taxi into town, and she had no desire to stand about for hours, waiting for Aristotle Myconos.

'*Kalimera, thespinis!*'

The waiter who had been observing her earlier had stepped into her path, and was looking down at her with evident admiration. He was a handsome young man, she had to admit, short and stocky like some Greeks, with bulging biceps visible through the sleeves of his thin cotton shirt. He was obviously well used to having success with the unmarried girls who stayed at the hotel, and the arrogance in his face reminded her painfully of that other occasion when she and her sister had accepted a similar invitation.

'*Kalimera,*' she said now, shortly, the tightness of her lips betraying her anger to more discerning eyes. '*Me sinhorite ...*'

'Ah!' The man's eyes widened at her casual use of his language. 'You are Greek?'

'No. I'm English,' retorted Martha coldly. 'Now—if you'll please get out of my way ...'

'*Poli kala ...*'

The Greek spread his hands expressively, and aware that they had attracted the attention of some of the other waiters, who were watching with amused eyes, Martha walked out of the dining room with burning cheeks.

On the verandah, however, her sense of humour asserted itself. It was ridiculous to get so worked up just because a young man had made a pass at her. What did it matter if he was Greek? It should be good to know that she was still attractive enough to warrant that kind of treatment on her first morning at the hotel, and she had no reason to feel oppressed by it. All the same, it had come too close on the heels of the thoughts that had plagued her during breakfast, and she walked uneasily along the balcony, aware of an increasing state of restiveness. She would be glad when it was ten o'clock, and she could get this interview with Dion's father over. It was a nerve-racking prospect, and not one she relished, and the determination she had felt in England to show Roger she had no qualms about meeting any of the Myconos family was rapidly waning. *Not* because she was afraid, she quickly told herself, but simply because she resented having to ask them for anything.

On impulse, she decided to go into town after all. She could always wander round the shops for a while, she thought reasonably. She needed some sun-tan oil. Her skin would quickly blister if she did not take the proper precautions, and that kind of discomfort she could do without.

She went back to her room first to check that her plain denim skirt and blue cotton shirt were suitable, and viewing her reflection in the mirror above the vanity unit, she wondered if her erstwhile father-in-law would notice the shadows beneath her eyes. The light make-up she wore did little to disguise the hollows where dark lashes swept the pale transparency of her cheeks, and she wished for once that she was not so slim. But the care of a five-year-old, an invalid, and a full-time job, was not designed to put flesh on her bones, and since her break-up with Dion, she had had little time to worry about her appearance. Only the heavy silken swathe of honey-coloured hair remained the same, a concession to vanity, and, confined in its single thick braid, an easy extravagance. There was seldom enough money for the luxury of a hairdresser, and Martha had grown used to washing her own hair and letting it dry naturally. Josy's hair, which Dion had found so unacceptable, was now almost as dark as his, although she had to admit that in other ways, her daughter was much more like herself.

Riding along the coast road in the taxi, Martha was glad her hair was confined. With all the windows open, the stiff breeze would quickly have disordered any hairstyle, but the few strands that blew across her pale forehead only added to her appearance, gentling the somewhat anxious severity of her expression.

'Mandraki?' enquired the driver over his shoulder, and Martha gathered her thoughts and nodded.

'*Efharisto*,' she agreed with a small smile, and the driver's brows lifted in silent approval. The smile erased the shadows from the wide grey eyes and brought an unconscious allure to features that in repose lacked that revealing candour.

Rhodes, or Rodos as the locals called it, was full of tourists. It was the start of the busiest season of the year, and the narrow streets were thronged with people. Open-air bars and *tavernas* were doing good business, and down by the harbour, there were the usual groups of older Greeks, gathered about the tables on the square, drinking the thick sweet Greek coffee, and arguing the politics of the day.

Martha tipped the driver and left the cab, walking across the road to where a handful of *caiques* were waiting to transport tourists to the tiny island of Khalki, or to Lindos, on the eastern coast of Rhodes, where the Acropolis attracted more and more visitors every year. She remembered visiting Lindos, and how she and Sarah had fallen about with laughter after jogging halfway up the hillside on donkeys.

Beyond the moorings, the harbour opened out to where

the iron deer, Rhodes' emblem, were perched on top of the harbour pillars. The mighty Colossus of Rhodes was supposed to have bestridden the entry years ago, one of the seven wonders of the ancient world, and without anything to remind one of the twentieth century, it was incredibly easy to imagine oneself back in another older time. Only a car ferry, steaming imperturbably across the horizon, destroyed the illusion, and Martha walked on to where the sea wall provided a buttress against the breeze.

It was nearing ten when she strolled back again, trying to ignore the butterflies in her stomach. She had occupied the last half hour by thinking of Josy, wondering what she was doing at playschool, and whether Sarah was coping in her absence. But now she was forced to think of her reasons for being here, and even to her ears they sounded suspect. It was going to be difficult to explain her gratitude to Roger, without Dion's father imagining their relationship to be something it was not. How could she expect him to understand that without Roger's friendship, she and her sister would never have been able to afford the flat they lived in? That Sarah depended upon him? She could not tell him about Sarah's accident; that was something too painful to contemplate. And besides, she shrank from any suggestion of appealing for sympathy. Dion must not think she wanted any charity from him or his family. All she hoped for was that Roger should be given the chance to excavate at Simos.

She had written to Aristotle Myconos deliberately. After all, the island belonged to Dion's father, it was the family estate, and the reason why Roger, and all other archaeologists, were refused permission to work there. Not that either Aristotle, or the members of his family, spent much of their time on Mycos. His shipping concerns meant he, and his three eldest sons, travelled the world quite extensively, and when he was not visiting the Myconos offices in New York or London or Tokyo, he was living in Athens, at his villa, which had a magnificent view of the Acropolis, within easy reach of his headquarters there.

The extent and complexity of the Myconos' wealth had always been a source of amazement to Martha. She liked money, of course she did, she liked spending it, but the extent to which money played a part in their lives had constantly bewildered her. Her needs had not been extravagant. Food to eat, clothes to wear, a car to drive—and even that had been a luxury, and not essential. It had always amused Dion that she had asked for so little, that she had been embarrassed when he offered her a trousseau from Balmain, or a necklace valued at several thousand pounds, from Tiffanys in New York. He had found it difficult to understand her apparent lack of ambition, the pride which forbade his desire to display her as his possession, and the lingering independence, which had ultimately led to their separation.

It was just as well, she acknowledged now, that she had not adapted too readily to that rarified atmosphere, that sybaritic way of life. It would have been far harder for someone without her streak of stubbornness, someone who had married for money, and not for love. Dion had never really believed that, she had realised long ago. He must always have suspected her feelings for him, been suspicious of her eagerness to become his wife. Deep inside, he had fostered jealousy and uncertainty, and she had finally come to the conclusion that he had confused love with a selfish desire for possession. His feelings had erupted on the night Josy was born, sweet innocent Josy, with that cap of russet-red hair, that had crystallised all Dion's suspicions into a hard core of distrust.

Aristotle Myconos's response to her letter had been brief. He refused, he said, to discuss any matter with her in a letter. If she wished to speak to him, she should come out to the islands, and much against her better judgment she had been forced to agree. Besides, she had argued, what could happen to her in Rhodes? She would meet her father-in-law, tell him of Roger's ambitions and the debt she owed to him, and hope that he would be generous. It was not so much to ask, surely. Roger and his assistant would not bring any disruption to their way of life. And it would be such a coup for the university if he could produce new evidence of what happened to the survivors of that ancient disaster.

The market, across the road from the harbour, was a meeting place for locals and tourists alike. Looking up an alleyway, Martha could see stalls, weighted down with oranges and peaches, and the enormous red and yellow melons, that were so much juicier than the fruit they bought back home. There were toy stalls and clothes stalls, stalls selling leather goods and pottery, and the exquisitely orna-mented dolls in traditional costume. She wondered if she ought to buy one of them for Josy, but she couldn't decide. Might it promote questions she was still not yet ready to answer? Josy had accepted the fact that she did not have a father without too much curiosity so far, but her daughter was an intelligent child, and Martha was constantly aware that sooner or later some more satisfactory explanation would be demanded. That was when the strength of her decision would be tested, and she acknowledged that deep inside her she had doubts as to whether she had the right to lie about the child's parentage. Since her agreement to speak to Aristotle Myconos on Roger's behalf, she had wondered whether this might be her opportunity to view the situation objectively, but every time she thought of offering Dion the right to share his daughter, a sense of panic gripped her. She loved Josy so much. Surely that was the important thing—not some nameless sum of money that offered security but nothing else! But if she gave Josy into her father's care, would the child be able to tell the difference?

She glanced at the watch on her wrist. It was after ten, she saw with some misgivings. The butterflies in her stomach responded with an increasing burst of activity, and she glanced about her anxiously, wondering whether she had mistaken the directions she had been given.

'Martha!'

The accented masculine tones made her heart skip a beat, and as she turned to face the man who had addressed her, her knees felt ridiculously weak. The similarity to Dion's voice was unmistakable, but to her intense relief the man confronting her was not her husband, but a stockier, younger facsimile.

'*Alex!*' Martha's voice betrayed her agitation, and she cast a worried look about her. 'Alex, what are you doing here?'

Dion's youngest brother surveyed her unsmilingly. He looked much older somehow than when she had last seen him, and although she realised that five years would have wrought some changes, Alex's transformation from an easy-going teenager into this serious-looking young man was quite startling. Gone were the jeans and sweat shirt, and in their place was an immaculate cream lounge-suit, and a matching silk shirt and tie. In her simple skirt and cotton shirt, Martha felt absurdly youthful, and she wished she had worn something more formal.

'Martha,' he said again, inclining his head, but making no move to kiss her, or shake her hand, or offer her any greeting other than his use of her name. 'If you will come with me . . .'

He gestured towards a sleek limousine that was waiting at the kerb a few yards further on, and Martha gave him a curious glance before saying doubtfully:

'Your father? He's waiting in the car?'

'Come.' Alex spread his hands politely. 'I will explain.'

Martha hesitated. 'Your father said he would meet me here,' she insisted, faint colour invading her cheeks as she realised he was not the ally he had once been. 'Alex, what's going on? Where is your father? Can't you at least tell me that?'

Alex pushed his hands into the pockets of his trousers, and rocked back and forth on his heels and toes. Then, with a sigh, he said: 'My father is not here, Martha. I am to take you to him. That is all. Now, will you come?'

Martha still resisted. 'Where is he?'

'Mycos. Where else?'

'Mycos!' Martha gasped. 'Oh, Alex, I can't come to Mycos!'

'You do not wish to see him?'

'Of course I do.' Martha's tongue appeared to moisten her lower lip. 'Alex, I arranged to meet your father in Rhodes. Not Mycos. I—well, visiting the island was not what we agreed.'

Alex shrugged, the dark brows drawn together over darker eyes. 'So you are refusing to come?'

'Alex, Mycos is at least five hours from here!'

'Not by air.'

'You have a plane?' she exclaimed, aghast.

'A helicopter,' he amended evenly. *'Endaksi?'*

'No! That is ...' Martha put an uncertain hand to her forehead, 'I would rather not meet your father at the villa.'

There was silence for a few moments after she had made this statement, a silence during which she became aware of the people going on with their lives around her, unaware of the intense upheaval she was suffering.

At last Alex spoke again. 'That is your final word?' he enquired. Then, after a pause: 'Dionysus went to Amsterdam—two days ago.'

Martha expelled her breath, hardly realising until that moment that she had been holding it. So she was not to meet with her husband. It was quite a relief. Despite what she had told Roger and Sarah, she had been apprehensive of seeing him again, not least because of the rawness of the wounds he had inflicted, and their vulnerability to any kind of abrasion. They were healed, but the scars remained, and she was not yet ready to test their strength.

Alex shifted his weight from one foot to the other, glancing expressively towards the car. He was growing impatient, and she had still to come to a decision.

'How long will your father be at the villa?' she asked, wondering whether she ought to telephone him, but Alex was not helpful.

'My sister Minerva is to be married in three days,' he declared. 'My father will be returning to Athens tomorrow for the wedding.'

'Minerva?' For a moment Martha was distracted. 'Little Minerva is getting married?' It hardly seemed possible.

'She is eighteen,' declared Alex flatly. 'In our country, marriage is the natural ambition of every woman.'

'Oh!' Martha accepted this with a rueful sigh. It was becoming increasingly obvious where Alex's sympathies lay, and no doubt in his eyes, she had committed an unforgivable sin by leaving her husband.

'*Etsi* . . .' He spread his hands now. 'What will you do?'

What could she do? Martha's palms were moist as she looped the strap of her bag over one shoulder. 'I'll come with you,' she said, and Alex strode away abruptly towards the car, swinging open the nearside door so that she could climb inside.

The car was chauffeur-driven, and, as Alex climbed in beside her and the windows were rolled up, air-conditioned. It was quite a relief to get out of the heat of the sun, and she remembered belatedly that she had not bought herself the oil for her skin as she had intended. Still, she would have little enough time to sunbathe today, and if all went well she would be returning to England tomorrow.

It was a good half hour to the airport, and realising she could not sit in silence for the whole of that time, Martha decided she would have to try and break down Alex's unnatural restraint. They had been such good friends. She couldn't believe he had condemned her so completely.

Turning towards him, she began by asking him whether he, too, was working for his father these days. 'I always thought you wanted to be a lecturer,' she commented. 'All that classical literature we used to read. Do you remember teaching me about Aeschylus and Sophocles, and how we used to act out those plays on the beach——'

'We all change,' Alex interrupted her shortly. 'We grow older—and wiser.'

Martha controlled the automatic rejoinder that sprang to her lips, and said instead: 'So you've given up your ideas of philosophy? You've decided that the material world has more to offer than the mythical one?'

Alex shifted impatiently in his seat. 'I do not think it matters to you what my opinions may be, Martha. I was a boy when you went away, now I am a man. That is all there is to it.'

'I see.' Martha made a negative gesture. 'In other words, I should mind my own business, hmm?'

Alex moved his shoulders dismissingly. 'You have not cared what has happened to us for five years. It is unreasonable to expect me to believe you care now.'

Martha accepted this broadside with a deep pang of regret. 'You may not believe this, but I have had my problems, too, you know,' she ventured. 'And as for our relationship—you were already planning on going to university. There was no way I could write to you without—without your brother and your father knowing. And in the circumstances I don't think that would have been a good idea, do you?'

Alex bent his head, pressing his lips together as he straightened the crease in his pants. He was obviously considering what she had said, but his loyalty to his brother, and to his family, was warring with the logic of his explanation.

'It has not been easy—for any of us,' he said at last, looking sideways at her. 'We have all to make our own judgment of events.'

'And what is your judgment?' asked Martha quietly.

Alex shook his head, and resumed his interest in his trouser leg. 'It is not up to me to say anything,' he replied at last. 'But I know what your leaving meant to my brother, and that I cannot forgive.'

Martha weathered this body blow with less fortitude. She had believed that of all of them, Alex might have kept an open mind. But it seemed he was as biased as the rest, and she did not look forward to this meeting with his father with any degree of anticipation.

A new airport had been built on Rhodes, far superior to the airport Martha remembered, whose approach between two hills had been a source of danger to larger aircraft. The new airport lay on the coast, to the south of the island, with a big new runway suitable to take the powerful jumbo jets that used it daily throughout the summer months.

The Myconos car was known to the airport staff, and they were passed through with the minimum of delay. The helicopter awaited them, and Alex dismissed the chauffeur before assisting Martha up the steps and into the aircraft.

She recognised the pilot. He used to help crew the ocean-going yacht that Aristotle kept moored at Piraeus, and it was strange to hear herself addressed as Madame Myconos once more. Dion had never petitioned for a divorce, and she had assumed he had waited to avoid the publicity it would undoubtedly attract, but she used her maiden name in England because it was easier that way.

She had never flown in a helicopter before. She seemed to remember a small hydroplane, but not a helicopter, and the curious lifting sensation she felt as they took off made her wish they had used the boat after all. Still, once they started moving forward, she forgot her fears, and the advantages it possessed over an aeroplane soon became evident. Flying at only several hundred feet instead of several thousand, she was able to distinguish the contours of every island they passed, and in her excitement she forgot that Alex had been offhand with her earlier.

'Isn't it tremendous?' she asked, raising her voice above the level of the engines. 'I mean, you can actually see how shallow the sea is in places. Oh, and look! Isn't that a dolphin down there? That black thing in the water?'

'I think it is more likely to be a fishing boat,' remarked Alex drily, unable to completely hide his amusement. 'We are not so low, you know. From this height a dolphin would hardly be visible.'

'Oh!' Martha pulled a rueful face, and for a moment Alex shared her disappointment. Then, quickly, he looked away again, but not before Martha had felt a slight uplift in her spirits. Given time, she was sure she could change Alex's opinion of her, and it was good to know that he still had a sense of humour.

There were sails below them now, white sails, pristine pure against the aquamarine water. They reminded Martha of the ketch Dion had sailed, and of weekends spent cruising these waters, far, in spirit at least, from the problems their marriage was facing.

'You're not married, Alex?' she enquired now, turning to look at her brother-in-law, and he shook his head.

'No,' he conceded, his voice almost inaudible beneath the throbbing of the propellers, and Martha guessed he was regretting his momentary lapse.

They were descending now, coming in low over the rocky contours of a headland, below which a narrow thread of sand glinted with burnished grains. There was a wooded hinterland rising to a barren summit, and then falling again more shallowly to a sheltered bay and a small harbour. The village, the island's only community, nestled round the bay, colour-washed cottages set in gardens bright with hibiscus and oleander. Martha could see the windmill that had once irrigated the terraces, where grapes grew with such profusion, and the deserted monastery of St Demetrius, high on the hillside. It was all so real and familiar, despite the absence of years, and once more she wondered how she could justify depriving Josy of this.

The Myconos villa was of typically Greek design. Palatial terraces, set about with gardens and fountains, and lily pools, thick with blossom. Marble pillars supported a first floor balcony, and shadowed the Italian tiles that covered the floor of the hall, and urns of flowering shrubs spilled scarlet petals across the veined mosaic of the entrance. Built on several levels, it sprawled among its pools and arbours, with all the elegant abandon of a reclining naiad.

A car took Martha and Alex from the landing field near the harbour, up the winding road to the villa. The chauffeur was another of the household staff, and like the pilot of the helicopter, he recognised his employer's daughter-in-law. Martha seemed to recall that his name was Spiros or Spiro, she wasn't certain which, but there had been so many names to remember, so many employees, who seemed to count it an honour to work for the Myconos family. And it was a family, in every sense of the word, a close-knit family, welded together by Aristotle Myconos' influence, where sons—and daughters-in-law, daughters—and sons-in-law, all came within the suffocating circle of his omnipotence. Maybe, if she and Dion had had a home of their own, things would have been different, she mused, and then squashed the thought. Aristotle had not been to blame for Dion's possessiveness, his absurd jealousy, his desire to confine his wife within the web of his family, and destroy all connections with her own ...

Nothing could prevent her nerves from tightening as the limousine turned between the stone gateposts of the villa. There were no iron fortifications here, as there were at the villa in Athens. No visible guards, no burglar-proof locks to keep out intruders. The main access to the island

was through the harbour, but just in case, Aristotle had the
coastline patrolled both day and night.

Thick shrubs hid all but the roof of the villa as the car
followed the winding curve of the drive, but eventually
they emerged before its white-painted façade, and Martha
saw again the imposing entrance of Dion's island home.
She remembered the first time she had seen it. She had
been enchanted then—enchanted and bemused, that a man
like Dionysus Myconos should want her for his wife.

The car stopped, and Alex thrust open his door to get
out. The chauffeur alighted and opened Martha's door, and
with a feeling of unease she stepped out on to the gravelled
forecourt.

It was slightly cooler here than in Rhodes, the soft
breeze bringing a pleasant relief in the heat of the day. Yet
the smell was the same, that tangy citrus smell, that
mingled here with the salty taste of the sea. And it was
quiet, so quiet after the noisy harbour at Rhodes, without
even the peal of voices to disturb the stillness. She had
thought Dion's older sister, Helene, might be there, with
her two sons, but there were no voices echoing from the
pool as there would have been if there were children about.

'My father is in his study,' Alex said, at her elbow, and
she looked up at him anxiously.

'Is no one else here?'

'You forget—I told you, my sister is getting married
on Friday. The family are gathering in Athens for the
celebrations.'

'Oh, yes.' Martha had forgotten. 'Well, shall we get it
over with?'

Alex raised his dark eyebrows, but he made no comment,
merely led the way beneath the marble pillars, and into
the cool, spacious hall.

Martha had forgotten the long windows at the back of
the hall, which gave a magnificent view of the curve of the
hillside, stretching up to the mellowed walls of the mon-

astery. The hall itself was on two levels, with an iron-railed balcony providing an oasis of plants in the heart of the building. Alabaster balusters supported the rail of the staircase, that curved to the upper storey, and overhead a crystal chandelier glinted dully below the arch of the ceiling.

Aristotle's study was some distance from the entrance hall, along corridors that gave tantalising glimpses of the sea between stone panels. The Aegean lay below them, somnolent in the noonday sun, a deeper blue than the sky above. It was so beautiful here, she thought with a pang. If only *people* were like places!

Her knees were knocking as they reached the leather-studded door, and in a spurt of panic she decided to dismiss any other motive she might have had for coming here. She would speak to Dion's father on Roger's behalf, and that was all. If he refused, she had done her best, and no one could do more. So far as her feelings towards Josy were concerned, they would have to wait. Maybe back in England, with the journey behind her, she would be able to view things less emotively, but right now she wanted to turn and run, and that was not the frame of mind in which to come to a rational decision.

Alex knocked, and then gave her a faintly appealing look. It was as if for a moment he regretted their estrangement as much as she did, and impulsively, she put her fingers on his arm taut beneath the fine material of his suit.

'I'm sorry,' she said, with a little rush of nostalgia. 'I did miss you, Alex—honestly!'

His lips were parting to make some response, when the door beside them opened. In that moment they were frozen in their adopted attitudes, caught for that fleeting split second in time, like two lovers planning an assignation. Then Martha's head turned, her hand dropped away, and her eyes widened in chilling disbelief as she gazed up at the man confronting them. This was not Aristotle Myconos, not this tall man, with thin, slightly haggard

eatures, and a lean, loose-limbed body. Aristotle was more
ike Alex, shorter, stockier, greyer—although this man's
dark hair was liberally sprinkled with that betraying fila-
ment. Besides, this man was younger, too young to have
sired four grown sons and two daughters, yet like Alex,
he too had suffered badly from the passage of years. His
eyes seemed darker, deeper-set, his cheeks hollower, his
frame more angular, thinner. This man was Dionysus
Myconos, her husband, yet not her husband, but the man
she had least wanted to meet.

CHAPTER TWO

SHE had misunderstood Alex's appealing look, she thought bitterly, trying to maintain some semblance of composure. It was sympathy, not understanding, she had glimpsed in his face, and she was tempted to turn on him angrily, scorning the lies he had told her to get her here. He had said Dion was in Amsterdam—*or had he*? All he had actually said was that he had gone there two days before.

'Will you not come in, Martha?' intoned her husband now, his voice as cold as the censure in his eyes. 'Alex, we will talk later.'

'Yes ...'

Alex turned away, but not before he had given Martha another of those reluctantly compassionate looks, though she was too intent on the interview ahead to notice it. With a stiffening of her backbone she stalked past her husband into the room, and then stopped short at the sight of her father-in-law, seated behind his square mahogany desk. Somehow she had expected Dion to be alone, and her step faltered as she heard her husband close the heavy door behind them.

'Martha!' Aristotle Myconos got heavily to his feet, and she saw he limped as he came round the desk to greet her. Like his sons he had aged, but although she eyed him warily, there was nothing but polite courtesy in his eyes. 'I am so glad you agreed to come here. As you can see, I am not so young as I used to be, and I leave most of the leg-work to my sons these days.'

'I'm sorry.' Martha's response was clipped, but she

couldn't help it. Whichever way she looked at it, she had been tricked, and she didn't like it.

'Please . . .' Aristotle indicated a dark green leather armchair, placed to one side of his desk. 'Will you not sit down? I realise you are feeling we have deceived you, but it was not reasonable for you to expect me not to tell Dion about your letter.'

Martha drew a deep breath. She was at a distinct disadvantage here. Before her was this old man, looking every one of his sixty-odd years, and behind her, boring into her shoulder blades, was the malevolent gaze of her husband. What was Dion doing here? What did he have to say to her? And why did she have the feeling she had been manipulated once again?

Composing her words carefully, she said: 'I told Alex I didn't want to come here. What we have to say to one another could have been said just as well in a letter——'

'Could it?'

The harsh tones that interrupted her were so unlike Alex's that Martha wondered how she could ever have mistaken them, however briefly. As she clutched her handbag as a sort of lifeline, Dion strode from the door to join his father, standing before the desk, feet slightly apart, arms folded across the muscled leanness of his chest. Like his brother and his father, he too was wearing formal clothes, but the dark colours he chose accentuated the alien cast of his skin, and clung to the narrow outline of his hips.

Facing him, Martha half wished he had remained where he was. In the years since their separation, she had succeeded in banishing his image to the farthest recesses of her mind, but now here he was again, tearing the veils aside, exposing her futile hopes and deepest fears.

'I wrote to your father because this is his island, and I hoped he might understand the position I was in,' she said now, realising she had to answer him. 'Roger—that is, Mr Scott—has—has been a good friend to—to us——'

'You mean—to you and your daughter?' enquired Dion coldly, and his father put a restraining hand on his arm.

'To—to Josy and me, yes. And—and to my sister.'

'Oh, yes, your sister,' Dion nodded. 'We must not forget her, must we?'

Martha drew a trembling breath and appealed to Aristotle, 'Is the answer no? Is that what you're about to tell me? Because if it is——'

'Will you not sit?' Aristotle gestured towards the chair again, and although the last thing Martha wanted to do in her husband's presence was to increase his advantage, she realised her father-in-law was finding the standing too much, and he would not sit down unless she did. With a hesitant little shrug she took the seat he offered, and with obvious eagerness he sought the relief of his own chair.

'Now,' he said, resting his palms on the desk, 'let us be honest with one another, hmm?'

'*Pateras!*'

'*Ohi*, Dionysus.' His father ignored his angry remonstrance. 'It must be said, and at once. It is not fair to keep the reasons for this interview from your wife. If, as you say, you wish to be free of this marriage, then it is right that Martha should understand from the outset.'

Martha could feel all the colour draining out of her cheeks at Aristotle's words. She had been shocked to see her husband, naturally, but it had not been entirely unexpected. *This was!* That Dionysus might be considering divorce had never entered her head. Not for years. And what was more, the idea was not even acceptable to her. *What about Josy?* she wanted to cry, but she didn't. She sat in frozen silence, trying desperately not to show how completely stunned she felt.

'So . . .' Aristotle surveyed her across the desk with quiet courtesy. 'You understand now why Dionysus is here. When you wrote to me concerning this matter of an archaeological survey, we took the opportunity to promote this meeting. These things are better said face to face. It has been in his mind for some time, I know, and your correspondence made it easier for us all.'

'I—I see.' Martha's mouth was horribly dry, and she had difficulty in articulating at all. 'And—and Roger's survey?'

'*Mou theos!*' snapped Dion angrily, even while Martha realised her words must sound incredibly foolish. But she couldn't bring herself to speak of anything else at this moment, and even his anger could not take away the feeling of disorientation that was gripping her.

'Be calm, my son.' Aristotle's controlled tones were a contrast to her husband's. 'Will you summon Andros? We all need a drink, I believe.'

While Dion crossed the floor and jerked open the door, Martha tried to get a hold on her emotions. But it wasn't easy with Aristotle's thoughtful eyes upon her, and without asking permission, she rose from her chair and crossed to the windows, staring out unseeingly at the terraced gardens below the villa. Dear God, she thought unsteadily, and she had thought Dion was there to make some demands upon her! She couldn't have been more wrong.

She heard the clink of glasses on a tray, and turned as Dion, accompanied by another manservant, re-entered the room. The man set the tray he was carrying on the desk, and bowed his head politely before making his departure. Then Dion crossed to the desk and with evident brusqueness asked her what she would like to drink.

There was lemonade there, and Martha picked that, unwilling to stretch her nerves any further by the introduction of alcohol. Dion and his father both chose gin, and her husband swallowed half his at a gulp before refilling his glass. As the chair she had been occupying was too close to the tray for comfort, Martha decided to perch on the window seat, and the cooling breeze the open window emitted helped to keep the faintness she was feeling at bay. This interview which had started so badly had suddenly got worse, and she had little confidence in her own ability to handle it.

'Now ...' Aristotle spoke again. 'First of all I suggest we clear up this matter of—Mr Scott? Is that right? Ah.' He nodded, as Martha agreed with his identification. 'I am sure you know, without my having to tell you, Martha, I never allow any historians to visit Mycos.'

'But that was not why you came, was it, Martha?' enquired her husband, with cold accusation, and with a shock she realised that there was more to this even now than she understood.

'I—I'm afraid——'

'Oh, please do not attempt to deceive us with your lies!' Dion grated angrily. 'You did not write to my father because you felt some—some philanthropic desire to help this man you speak of.'

'Then why did I write?' she found herself asking, unable to prevent the question from spilling from her tongue, and once again it was Aristotle Myconos who tried to cool the situation.

'Dionysus, let us not jump to conclusions,' he said, and there was a warning in his eyes that Martha failed to comprehend. 'Let Martha tell us her reasons. Then we can discuss this matter.'

'I've told you my reason,' she exclaimed, coming to her feet again. 'What other reason could there be?'

Dion's narrow lips curled. 'You did not consider perhaps that, now the child is older, it might be possible for you to sue for maintenance?'

'Maintenance?' Martha was horrified. '*No!* No, of course not.'

'Dion ...' Again that warning note in his father's voice, but this time he ignored it.

'I should tell you,' he said coldly, 'I have been to England. I have seen the circumstances in which you live.

And it is no surprise to me that you have finally decided that independence is not everything you thought it to be.'

His words temporarily numbed Martha. Dion had been to England! He had seen the circumstances in which she lived! What did that mean? Had he seen Josy? Did he know about Sarah? His next words enlightened her.

'You have not sued for divorce. This man, whoever he is, has not made any apparent effort to marry you, to father the child he seeded in you. You must be getting desperate to give the child a name!'

'You are wrong,' she declared now. 'Totally and utterly wrong! I—I—if you think Roger is—is Josy's father, then you're crazy!'

Dion took a step towards her at this piece of insolence, but as if mindful of his father's watching presence, he halted. 'Then who is he? Tell me that?' he demanded. 'And tell me why you dared to write to my father asking for a permission you knew would be denied you!'

Martha's breathing was shallow and uneven, but she managed to say what she had to. 'After—after I left you, I stayed with Sarah for a while, but her flat was tiny, just a bed-sitter, and her landlady didn't take too kindly to having a baby's nappies hanging in the bathroom. Then—then——' She broke off, still unwilling to give him the satisfaction of knowing about Sarah's accident, and of how useless the flat had become to someone confined to a wheelchair, and went on less convincingly: 'We needed somewhere else, somewhere I—I could wheel a pram. Roger offered us the ground floor of his house.'

Dion regarded her through lowered lids. 'Why should he do that?'

'Would you believe—kindness?'

Dion's lips thinned. 'You ask too much.'

'Obviously.' Martha held up her head. 'Well, if that's all there is to say ...'

'It is not.' Dion cast brooding eyes in his father's direction. 'There are still things we have to say to one another.'

His father rose abruptly to his feet. Pushing back his chair, he came round the desk, but when Martha began to accompany him to the door, he waved her back again, saying:

'You will eat lunch with us before you leave, Martha. You must be hungry. I will go and speak with Maria myself.'

'Oh, no—please—I mean——' Martha glanced awkwardly at her husband. 'I think it would be better if I left right away.'

'You forget, there is still the matter of the divorce to discuss,' put in Dion bleakly, and his father bowed his head politely and left the room, alone.

With his departure, Martha felt an increasing weight of tension. Dion in his father's company was barely tolerable, Dion alone was terrifying. It wasn't that he frightened her exactly, although his anger did send frissons of apprehension along her spine, but she was afraid of the power he had over her, the dark power that both attracted and repelled, and which had driven her to the very edge of sanity during those first weeks after she had left him.

Dion, for his part, seemed curiously loath to break the silence that had fallen between them, and while Martha sipped nervously at her lemonade, her eyes darting anxiously about the room, he walked heavily over to the windows and stared indifferently out to sea. She thought he was composing how next he might humiliate her, and she was shocked when he asked suddenly:

'Why did you do it, Martha? Why did you leave me? Did I ask you to go? Did I threaten you with divorce? If this man meant so much to you, why did you not tell me before the child was born?'

Martha put her glass down carefully on the corner of

the desk, and then, arming herself with what little composure she had left, she said: 'You know why I left you, Dion. You couldn't possibly expect me to stay with you after the things you said. I may not have the Myconos money, but I do have some pride, and no one——' her voice cracked ignominiously, '—no one, least of all my husband, is going to call me a tramp and get away with it!'

'*Poli kala*, what would you call it?' he demanded, turning then to face her, his eyes narrowed and provoked. 'How was I supposed to react? Should I have said—of course, I understand about these things! It is *natural* that my wife— *my liberated English wife*—should need the admiration of more than one man! *No!*'

Martha drew an uneven breath. 'It's hopeless. You're unreasonable! You just won't listen——'

'Oh, *parndon*!' His features were hard and angry. 'But what am I supposed to listen to? More lies? More evasions? You dare to come here pleading for this man, knowing you are causing nothing but pain and embarrassment to me and my family, and you think *I* am unreasonable!'

Martha sighed. 'Roger Scott is a family friend,' she said wearily. 'Just a family friend.'

Dion left the window to join her by the desk, regarding her coldly as she stood her ground. 'And is he the father of your child?' he asked bleakly. 'This *family* friend?'

'No!'

Martha's denial was automatic, but she realised as she spoke that it might have been simpler not to answer him. She was getting into deep water, and until she had had time to think about the divorce, time to consider what she was going to do about Josy, she should not make such unequivocal statements.

'Then who?' Dion was relentless. 'Someone in London, that I know. Someone your sister introduced you to, perhaps? She never wanted you to marry me, did she? That was never in her scheme of things. She would enjoy hurt-ing me through you, wouldn't she?'

Martha gasped. 'That's a rotten thing to say! And it's not true. Sarah's not like that. She cares about me, that's all. She knew that money was your god, and she was afraid I might be stifled by it. She wanted me to be happy, but she was not to blame for our incompatibility.'

Dion's face darkened ominously. 'We were not incom-patible!' he declared angrily. 'At least, not before *she* interfered.'

Martha trembled with indignation. 'You could always find excuses for your own inadequacy, couldn't you, Dion?' she taunted, and then gulped convulsively as his hands fastened on her upper arms.

'Have a care what you say to me, Martha,' he grated harshly. 'You are my wife still, and in my country that counts for a little more than it does in yours!'

'Are you threatening me, Dion?'

She squared her shoulders bravely, but the pressure of his fingers through the thin cotton of her shirt was agonis-ing. She would have bruises there tomorrow, she thought tremulously. Dion did not know his own strength, and once she would have gloried in the raw passion of his nature. But now she was aware of so many other things, of the savagery in his face, and the anger in his voice, of the power he pos-sessed to destroy her at will, and the painful awareness that he was the only man who could make her run the whole gamut of so many conflicting emotions.

He looked down at her and saw the apprehension in her face, the uneasy anticipation of what form his retribution might take, and a low groan escaped him. He had never struck a woman, and despite the chasm that yawned be-tween them, he could not strike her now. His eyes, boring into hers, clouded with impatience, and her lips parted to allow a tiny gasp of relief to escape her.

'I should kill you!' he muttered, his teeth grating together. 'You tell me you do not want a child yet, that it is too soon, that we need time to be alone together, before we assume such a responsibility. And I agree with you! I am happy to have you to myself——'

'To *possess* me,' put in Martha unevenly, and winced as his fingers tightened.

'*Etsi*—to possess you, as you say,' he agreed harshly. 'And was not that possession to your liking also?'

'Dion, please . . .' Martha's cheeks flushed, but he ignored her.

'No matter,' he said, his lips twisting. 'The truth is, you betrayed me with another man, you let him give you the child that you denied me. And for that you deserve more than my contempt!'

Martha shook her head. 'There's no point to this discussion——'

'Is there not?' His eyes narrowed. 'Why should you care if I enjoy—torturing myself in this way?'

Martha tried to twist away from him, but it was to no avail, and with a feeling of desperation she exclaimed: 'You're not torturing yourself, Dion. You're torturing me! You're hurting me! Will you please let go of my arms?'

'Why should I?' Instead of doing so, he jerked her towards him, and now she could feel the bones of his legs against her shaking knees, could smell the clean masculine aroma of his body, mingling with the heat of his breath. 'I have anticipated this moment since your letter to my father arrived. I wanted to hurt you, to humiliate you, to see your disappointment when we saw through your puny schemes.' He paused, his eyes dropping briefly to the panting rise and fall of her breasts. 'And I wanted to see how the years had treated you, to see whether you had suffered, as you made me suffer!'

'Dion!'

She gazed up at him helplessly, conscious that against her will, he was arousing her awareness of him as a man, a man moreover who had been her husband, and who had once been able to weaken her limbs by the simple exchanging of a glance. She didn't want to remember these things, she didn't want to acknowledge that instinctive attraction between them, that had torn down the barriers of race and society, and made them both prisoners of its urgent expression. It was not love, it had never been love, on his part at least, she exhorted herself, but that didn't prevent the devastating effect he was having on her senses.

'The child?' he muttered huskily, holding her eyes with his. 'Is she like you? Does she have your colouring? Your slenderness? Your determination?'

Martha trembled, pressing her hands against her chest, keeping them away from him with a supreme effort of will power. 'Y-yes,' she admitted at last, 'she is like me. She's quite tall for her age, and slender, and she does have a very definite will of her own.'

He nodded, slowly, his mouth taking on a downward curve, as remorse twisted his expression. 'I knew she would,' he averred hoarsely, as the hostility faded from his eyes to be replaced by a tormented bitterness. 'Your daughter was bound to be like you. Just as wilful, just as independent, and just as *beautiful* . . .'

Martha's breath caught in her throat. There was no mistaking the violent emotion that dragged that word from his lips, and she was scarcely surprised when their mutual awareness became too much for him, and with a moan of self-disgust, he brought her body close to his. She could not avoid touching him now. Her hands were crushed against the hardness of his chest, only lightly disguised beneath the maroon silk of his shirt, and as his hands slid down her spine, she could feel the stirring muscles of his thighs.

It was his mouth that truly possessed her, parting her lips beneath its moist invasion, exploring and searching and inspiring a response that she had no will to resist. Maybe if she had had more time, she thought, hanging on to coherence with only a shred of control, if she had been prepared for the effect he would have on her. But she would never have believed that he could do this to her, and all the old magnetism came flooding back, to envelop her in a drowning web of sensual feeling. The pressure increased, became passionate, enfolding them both for a spell in hungry, mindless abandon. His hands were on her thighs, arching her body, moulding her to his maleness with an ease born of their knowledge of one another. And she wanted him, she realised. Wanted him so badly there was a physical ache inside her, as there had been in those awful weeks after she left him.

'Martha,' he groaned, releasing her mouth to seek the scented hollows behind her ear. 'Who is the father of your child? Don't I have the right to know?' and in the emotive tenor of the moment, she betrayed herself completely and whispered huskily:

'*You are!*'

His withdrawal was so abrupt, it left her bemused and speechless, staring at his contorted face without really understanding why he looked so balefully furious.

'*Theos!*' he grated disbelievingly. '*Mou theos!* Say it is not so?'

Martha blinked, and put a dazed hand to her head. It was difficult to bring her mind to normal things, when every nerve and tissue in her being was still crying out for a satisfaction it had not received. Her hair felt reasonably tidy, she thought unsteadily, and her fingers fumbled to fasten the button of her shirt which had come loose in their ardent exchange. Her face was probably bare of all make-up, but that didn't really matter, although her lips felt bruised from the hungry pressure of his. What did matter was that somehow he had tricked her once again, and this whole fiasco had been staged to discover the truth behind Josy's conception. It was cold and ruthless, but typical of the man he had become, and she felt soiled and abused, and totally abased.

'*Martha!*' He was speaking to her again, but she refused to answer him, turning away, picking up her handbag which had fallen to the floor, extracting her handkerchief to scrub the taste of his lips from her mouth.

'Martha!' His response to her ignoring of him was to snatch the bag and the handkerchief out of her hands, throwing them to the floor with a cold disregard for their well-being. 'Martha, I demand an answer!'

She backed away from him, too stunned to say anything. He had seduced her into betraying herself, and her thoughts ran wildly in all directions, seeking escape from the awful implications of the situation. Did he believe her? How could he not, when she had confessed so emotionally? She had sworn he would never get that information from her, not unless she had chosen to tell him, and now he had cajoled it from her, in the most degrading circumstances ever.

The study door opened suddenly and Aristotle re-appeared. His shrewd dark eyes took in the scene he had interrupted—his son's grim countenance, Martha's pale desperation, and the handbag and square of linen lying like a gauntlet on the floor between them. Then, with the discretion born of years of boardroom diplomacy, he said calmly:

'A cold buffet has been prepared. Martha ...' he addressed the young woman holding weakly to the back of a chair, 'if you would like to come with me ...'

Martha wanted to refuse him. She did not want to take anything from the Myconos family. But it was an escape from Dion, from the suffocating menace of his presence, and with a little helpless shrug of her shoulders she turned towards the door.

The corridor stretched ahead of her, endlessly, and as

if sensing her uncertainty, Aristotle offered his arm. 'Come,' he said. 'My son will follow. We will walk together, and you can tell me about your life in England, and about that sister of yours of whom you were so fond.'

It was a polite way of gaining her compliance and Martha, much against her better judgment, took his arm, and they walked slowly down the cool, arched passageway. When Helene's boys were here, or Nikos, with his family, these halls rang with the excited laughter of children, but today they were cloistered, quiet, echoing the brooding violence of Dion's anger.

It was a relief to get outside, beneath the perspex awning, whose slatted leaves shaded the noonday sun. The scent of mimosa mingled with the perfume of the flowering vines that overhung the trellises, and the blue-green tiles of the swimming pool, were visible between their blossoming stems. A circular, glass-topped table was set with dishes of meats and salads, savoury eggs and stuffed tomatoes, lobster and anchovies, and various other Greek dishes, that Martha had once found much to her taste. There was a jug of freshly-squeezed orange juice, and another of grapefruit juice, and tall frosted glasses beside a bucket of ice containing a bottle of champagne. She had forgotten Aristotle's love for champagne, she realised, trying to concentrate on the moment, and dreading the inevitable dénouement that Dion was sure to make.

'Kathiste, parakalo,' Andros invited politely, moving from his stance beside the table to offer Martha a chair, and she sank into it gratefully.

'Thank you,' she said, giving him the benefit of a wavering smile, and his eyes warmed her after the cold brilliance of Dion's.

Aristotle seated himself opposite her, and while Andros offered the various dishes for Martha's selection, he opened the champagne. The cork burst from the neck of the bottle, but he caught the Dom Perignon expertly in his glass, raising the frothy wine to his lips, and toasting her in its potency.

Martha accepted only a slice of ham flavoured with honey from the slopes below Parnassus, and a little of the Greek salad, that mainly comprised huge slices of tomato and cucumber, tossed in a little light oil. She was not hungry, but she was feeling a little faint, and she hoped the food might restore her equilibrium. Right now, she felt confused and unbalanced, and completely incapable of anticipating what might happen next.

Dion appeared as she was sipping a glass of orange juice. She had refused Aristotle's offer of champagne, realising anything alcoholic might aggravate the sense of unreality that was gripping her, but her husband's appearance had an intoxicating mesmerism all its own. She felt like a rabbit, hypnotised by a snake, her limbs frozen into attitudes of helplessness and supplication.

'Ah, Dionysus! We were beginning to wonder if you intended to join us,' his father observed, with mild acerbity. 'As you can see, we have started without you. Will you have some champagne? Or would you prefer a less stimulating substitute, like Martha?'

Dion's glance flickered over his wife's bent head, and then he walked to where a low stone wall provided a man-made barrier between the patio area and the terraces that fell away gently below them. He leant against the low wall, resting his hips on its weather-worn stones, and ignoring his father's offer of refreshment, he said:

'Where is Alex? I wanted to speak with him.'

Martha's nerves stretched as she heard Aristotle explaining that his youngest son was waiting for a telephone connection to Athens. 'There has been some difficulty in getting through,' he remarked, moving his shoulders in an offhand gesture. 'And I wanted those figures from Stavros for you to work on this evening.'

'Mmm.' Dion's response was less enthusiastic, and listening to him, Martha waited in agonised expectation for him to tell his father what he had just learned. But he didn't. Instead, he left the wall to take a seat at the table, near enough to Martha for her to be constantly aware of him, but not near enough to intimidate her.

'*Endaksi.*' His father handed him a glass of champagne, and dismissed Andros with a flick of his fingers. 'Now, you can tell me what you have decided.'

Martha looked down at her plate, pushing the ham round with her fork, but Dion did not immediately reply. He leant across the table and helped himself to a circle of toast, liberally spread with the dark brown roe his father found so palatable, and then, with his mouth full, he queried in a muffled voice: 'About what, in particular?'

Aristotle's greying brows descended, and for the first time since Martha had joined them he displayed a little of the Myconos temper he normally controlled so well. 'You know the subject to which I am referring, my son,' he essayed brusquely. 'What arrangements have you made? Did you explain to Martha that the settlement need not be ungenerous, in spite of all the circumstances, providing she does not defend the suit, *ne*?'

Dion took a taste of his champagne, emptied his mouth, and then rubbed his lips on the back of his hand. 'I think I need more time to consider the matter,' he said finally, leaning back in his chair, and studying the sparkling liquid in his glass with thoughtful deliberation. 'You understand, Papa?'

'You are saying that Martha has refused to give you a divorce?' Aristotle demanded, in ominous tones, and Martha, bewildered by this unexpected turn of events, hastened to deny it.

'We didn't discuss—divorce,' she said tightly, unwilling to suffer the suspense any longer. 'We spoke about——'

'—many things,' broke in Dion sharply, cutting her off before she could commit herself. 'Enough to know there is more to the destruction of a marriage than a few words written on a sheet of paper!'

'*Dionysus!*' His father rose to his feet with quivering dignity. 'What are you saying? What foolishness is this? What hold does this woman have over you, that you cannot be in her presence for more than fifteen minutes without you change the decision of weeks—months! Have done with it! Do not allow her to bewitch you once again. Make the incision! Break loose from those chains that have bound you to the past for five long years!'

Martha was trembling as he spoke. She had guessed Dion's father had only tolerated her for his sake, and she had known of the initial opposition both his parents had raised to their marriage. Yet their love had seemed so strong then, so worthy of any strains which might be put upon it. That was before she learned of the demands the Myconos corporation put upon its executives, before she had found herself alone for days—weeks—on end, with Dion at one side of the world and herself at the other. Of course, even that would not have been so bad if she had been free to do as she wanted. But she was not. She was expected to conform, like all the other Myconos wives, and her prevailing streak of stubborness and independence had eventually been her downfall ...

She came back to the present with a start to find Dion was on his feet too now, and although the exchange he was having with his father had reverted to their own language, Martha was able to understand most of what was being said.

'You overreach yourself, Papa,' her husband was stating bleakly, subjecting his father to the same piercing scrutiny she had suffered earlier. 'I take care of my own affairs, and you would do well to remember it. You are not my counsel, nor are you my keeper. You are my father, and as such, I offer you my respect. I appreciate that your opinions may

differ from mine, but do not make the mistake of thinking
that because I listen to you, I think as you do. I am no
longer a child, Papa. I am a man. I heed advice—but I
make the decisions, you understand?'

The lines on Aristotle's face had become more deeply
drawn as Dion spoke, and although he drew himself up to
his full height, he was still several inches shorter than his
son. Martha, tense and nervous as she was, could still find
it in her heart to feel sorry for him, and she realised with a
pang that her husband had changed more than she had ever
imagined. Once he would not have contradicted his father,
would not have argued with him, or denied him the right to
state his opinions, would not have used his superior wit and
intelligence to make the old man appear frailer than he
actually was. This man was harder, shrewder, more ruthless, every inch the arbiter of his fate, and that of the
Myconos corporation, and Martha realised that while his
father might still nominally hold the reins, Dion had inherited in everything but name.

'So,' his father said now, resting his palms upon the
table. 'Does not your wife—does not Martha have any
choice in this?' He turned to his daughter-in-law, and
spread his hands. 'Dare I say that I cannot believe she
wants to prolong this situation?'

'Martha and I will have plenty of time to talk of this,' declared Dion abruptly, without even glancing at his wife. 'I
intend to have her belongings collected from her hotel in
Rhodes, and——'

'No!' It was Martha who interrupted now, struggling to
her feet and facing him defensively. 'There is nothing to
discuss, Dion. The situation was—was decided for us. Five
years ago! I came here to speak to your father, and I've
done so. That's all. I'll leave as soon as the helicopter is
ready to take me.'

'If you insist.' Dion's indifference was disturbing. 'But
we are going to talk, Martha. Whether you wish it or not.'

His eyes held hers. 'Either here or at your hotel, it makes no difference to me. But remember, you came here of your own free will. And I should consider your proverb about fools and angels, before you say any more.'

CHAPTER THREE

MARTHA'S lips quivered. 'I think you're trying to frighten me, Dion,' she said unevenly.

'Do you think that?'

'Yes.'

He shrugged, and while she watched, he slipped his hand into his inside pocket. For one awful moment she thought he was about to pull a gun on her. He had carried one occasionally in the old days, for protection only, when circumstances demanded it, and she had always been repelled by its cold, metallic accuracy. But, as her palms moistened in opposition to the dryness of her mouth, he drew out a narrow cigar case, and flicking it open, took out one of the slim panatellas he favoured. He put it between his teeth and then said calmly:

'My sister is getting married on Friday. My father and I must return to Athens for the wedding. But I shall be back here on Saturday night, and we will continue this discussion then. It is up to you whether you choose to bear the cost of an hotel room, or make use of the villa in my absence. Either way, we will talk further on Saturday.'

'But I can't stay here until Saturday!' protested Martha. 'I—why—I have to get back. I have a job, and—and there are things I have to see to.'

'You mean—the child?' enquired Dion sombrely.

Martha licked her lips. 'Among other things, yes.'

'Cannot your sister—cannot *Sarah* cope?'

Martha hesitated. 'No. No, she can't.'

'Why not? Is one child so hard to handle?'

Martha sighed. 'I have my reasons.'

'So.' Dion drew an impatient breath, pulling out a lighter and applying it to the tip of his cigar. Then he glanced at his father. 'It seems I must offer my regrets to Andreas and Minerva.'

'No!'

Martha's instinctive denial was only narrowly forestalled by his father's, as Aristotle gazed disbelievingly at his son.

'You cannot mean to deny your sister the happiness of your company on her most special day!' he declared. 'She would never forgive you. You know how much she depends on you—of all her brothers! I will not—I *cannot* beg you too strongly to reconsider, Dionysus.'

Martha felt an intense weariness overtaking her. This had all been too much for her. First Dion's appearance, then his talk of divorce; the scene in his father's study was almost too painful to consider, but it had happened, and now he was playing this cat-and-mouse game of secrets. Just what did he intend to do? How could she interfere in family matters? Aristotle was looking at her as if she was the only person capable of changing his son's mind, but how could she stay in Rhodes when Sarah was depending on her to return?

'I have to get back,' she insisted unsteadily, avoiding her father-in-law's reproachful gaze. 'I'm sorry, but I must.'

Dion absorbed this for a few moments, drawing deeply on his cigar, then he seemed to come to a decision. '*Poli kala*,' he essayed firmly. 'You will fly back to London to-morrow, *ne*, and return here on Saturday, bringing the child with you.'

Aristotle was looking at his son now as if he had suddenly taken leave of his senses, but Martha was shaken by the realisation that in a way she had played right into his hands. Panic soured the orange juice inside her, and bile rose in a nauseating surge to the back of her throat.

'I—I can't do that,' she stammered, wondering desperately what the laws of paternity were in Greece, and whether, if she brought Josy here, she would be allowed to take her home again, but Dion was adamant.

'Why not?' he demanded, and only she understood the challenge in his words. 'You said yourself that your sister could not cope with the child. I am offering you a solution, that is all.'

Martha shook her head. 'I—I couldn't possibly afford——' she began, grasping at the expense like a drowning swimmer clutches at a blade of grass, but Dion had all the answers.

'The tickets will be arranged for you,' he said smoothly. 'And now, if you are ready to leave, I myself will drive you back to the helicopter.'

'No! That is——' Martha gazed appealing at Aristotle Myconos, but he could not—*or would not*—help her. Dion was already moving towards the house, preparatory to summoning the car, when she realised she would have to use Sarah after all. 'I can't return to Rhodes, because Sarah needs me.'

She saw her husband's expression change as she brought her sister's name into it. Dion had never liked Sarah, and in all honesty, Sarah had not encouraged him to do so. In the beginning, Martha had found her sister's attitude towards her husband rather irritating, but as their relationship foundered she began to see that Sarah had been right all along.

She and Sarah had been very close in those days before her marriage. Their parents had been quite old before they started their family, and after their father's death twelve years ago, their mother had found it difficult to carry on. Consequently, when Martha was sixteen and Sarah was eighteen, they found themselves orphaned, and more dependent on each other than ever.

Nevertheless they were good friends, and once Martha had completed her secretarial training and got a job as a doctor's receptionist, they had found no difficulty in keeping up the small house in Wimbledon, where they had lived all their lives. Until that holiday in Rhodes, which had altered everything ...

Now, Dion removed his cigar from his mouth and said flatly: 'I see. I should have known your sister would be involved in some way. Very well. Why does she need you? Because she is afraid of your becoming involved with this family again?'

'Dion!' Alex's urgent voice interrupted them, and turning, Martha saw her husband's brother beckoning from the open doorway. 'Dion, Giorgios is on the telephone. He wishes to speak to you personally.'

The oath Dion uttered made Martha flinch, and she watched apprehensively as he flung down his cigar and ground it under his heel. Then, with a frustrated gesture, he strode across the patio, and disappeared into the house.

However, when Alex would have followed his brother, his father's voice arrested him. 'Martha is leaving,' Aristotle said, the firmness of his tone belied by the unsteady movement of the hands he extended towards her. 'That is what you wish to do, is it not?' he adjured, waiting expectantly for her reply, and dry-mouthed she nodded. '*Kalos!* You will drive her to the helicopter, Alexander.'

'But—my handbag——'

Martha's words were faltering, her head curiously light at this unexpected reversal of the situation, and for a moment Aristotle's impatience showed. Then, gesturing towards Alex, he bade him collect her belongings from his study, while he escorted his daughter-in-law to the car.

The limousine was waiting where she had left it, and the old man saw her comfortably seated before glancing round irritably as the minutes stretched. Martha, too, was aware of the tension that was gripping him, and while she knew she must take this chance of escape, she couldn't help wondering whether she was not simply aggravating Dion's reactions.

'Your son——' she began, looking up at her father-in-law, and Aristotle turned back to her with assumed dignity.

'Dionysus will have time to reconsider his position,' he replied doggedly, his breath escaping on a sigh of relief as Alex re-appeared. '*Herete*, Martha. Go with God!'

It was a nerve-racking journey down to the helicopter. Any minute Martha expected to hear a fast car speeding behind them, or some dramatic summons on the two-way radio incorporated in the front console. But nothing happened. The helicopter took off, and as they circled the island, she saw no sign of activity from the villa, not even the puff of dust from the road which might have indicated a fast-moving vehicle.

Alex did not accompany her back to her hotel. He made his farewells at the airport, and she thanked him for returning her safely.

'We will meet again,' he averred gently, shaking her hand in parting, and she wondered why he sounded so sure of himself. But she was not going to ask him. She was only too relieved to be back on neutral ground again, and she climbed into the back of the car that awaited her with scarcely concealed relief.

Back at the hotel, however, reaction overtook her, and she went up to her room to fling herself on the bed, feeling totally and completely shattered. It had been the most exhausting episode of her whole life, and she wondered apprehensively what Dion would do now. It was of a certainty that he would not give up, not so easily, and while his father had his own reasons for wanting her gone, he did not know the whole truth of what had happened.

Taking that particular incident into consideration, Martha tried to view what had happened with an objective eye. It wasn't easy. Her emotions were still too painful, too raw, too sensitive to the humiliation she had suffered. She had despised him before, she felt she hated him now—and hated herself too, for the disgusting way she had betrayed herself.

How could she have acted that way? How could she have been taken in by that plea for sympathy, that deliberate arousal of her compassion, that had ended in her stumbling confession? It sickened her to think of how easily he had deceived her, and how weak she had been, accepting his kisses and the intimacy of his embrace, only to find she had been used for his purpose.

With a groan of frustration she sat up, crossing her legs and balling her knuckles into fists. There was no point in belabouring the issue. What was done was done. She had been a fool to think she could deal with the Myconos's like normal people. They were not *normal* people. They were jealous of their power, possessive of the things—*and people* —they considered theirs, and totally insensitive to anyone's needs but their own. It had been *her* conceit which had made her imagine she could walk into the lions' den, and come out unscathed. Why had she done it? Just to help Roger? Or because, as Josy grew older, she had felt some constraint to tell the child's father the truth? Maybe she would have told Aristotle, allowed him to decide whether his son should be told, but she had never imagined being faced with the difficulties she faced now.

Sliding off the bed, she padded on to the balcony, flopping into a wrought iron chair, and looking at that splendid view, which earlier in the day had given her such a feeling of reassurance. It didn't reassure her now. All she could think of was how stupid she had been, how childish and how gullible, and how uncertain the future looked at this moment.

Despite her apprehensions, Dion did not try to contact her

before she returned to London, and she couldn't decide whether she was glad or sorry. It was typical of him that he should keep her in suspense like this, and Martha half wished she had not run away from Mycos, and given him such an advantage.

It was June, and the holiday season, and Heathrow was a hive of activity when she landed there the following afternoon. She lugged her suitcase on to the tube, and rode into Central London that way, but changing trains for Wimbledon, she managed to get her ankles snagged by a carelessly placed pushchair. By the time she had walked the quarter mile from the station to Meredith Road, she was feeling distinctly strained, and it didn't help to find Josy playing, without supervision, in the garden at the front of the house, her dress and sandals stained with muddy water.

'Mummy!' The little girl was completely unaware of her mother's irritation, and flung herself into Martha's arms, with all the loving impulsiveness of her nature. 'You're back!' she exclaimed, hugging her tightly. 'I've missed you!'

'I've missed you, too, darling,' said her mother gently, unwilling to remonstrate with her the minute she returned home. 'But where is Auntie Sarah—or Mrs Bennett? You know you're not supposed to play outdoors alone.'

'I know.' Josy wrinkled her nose. 'But I was tired of playing in the bedroom, and it was such a lovely day.'

'Why couldn't you play in the living room?' Martha objected, and then added: 'Where is Mrs Bennett? I suppose Auntie Sarah's lying down, isn't she?'

'Yes.' Josy accompanied her mother up the path and into the tall Victorian house Roger had inherited from his parents. 'But Mrs Bennett's gone home, and I——'

'Gone home?' her mother interrupted her blankly. Mrs Bennett shouldn't have gone home. Not at four o'clock in the afternoon anyway. She had agreed to take Josy to her play group in the mornings, collect her again at one o'clock, and stay until after their evening meal. 'Oh, lord! What's been going on?'

The hall of the house was dark and rather gloomy, redolent of shadowy corners and stained paint. Roger hadn't bothered to have it decorated for years, and Martha had enough to do, keeping their rooms in reasonable order.

Their apartment, if it could be called such, comprised a living room and kitchen, where they took most of their meals, two bedrooms, one for Sarah, and the other which Martha shared with her daughter, and a tiny bathroom that was across the hall. All on one level, it was easy for Sarah to wheel herself from room to room, and although there was no garden at the back of the house, only a small yard, they had had a concrete slope installed, which meant that she could get outdoors that way. As the buildings were semi-detached, it was a simple matter for her to wheel herself round to the front of the house, and the independence this had given her more than made up for its lack of modern amenities.

Entering the living room, Martha was forcibly struck by its shabbines after the opulent appointments of the Myconos villa. Even the hotel in Rhodes had been luxurious compared to this, and her heart sank when she saw the stack of dishes in the kitchen sink, and smelled the rank odour of congealing food from plates still residing on the table. Had anyone done anything since she went away? she wondered, confused by Mrs Bennett's absence. She was usually so reliable, when it came to looking after Josy, and she had been paid to prepare their evening meal while Martha was away.

'It's a mess, isn't it?' remarked the little girl, with childish candour, and Martha felt a reluctant smile tugging at her lips.

'Yes, it is,' she agreed, putting down her suitcase, and taking off the jacket of her pants suit. 'Get me that plastic apron, will you, darling? While I'm washing these, you can tell me what's happened to Mrs Bennett.'

Josy obediently passed her mother the apron, and then carried a stool to the sink, to enable her to perch on the end of the draining board. But when Martha's hands were plunged deep into the soapy suds, she surprised her mother by saying thoughtfully:

'I don't think Mrs Bennett likes Auntie Sarah. Do you?'

Martha frowned, concentrating in scouring the grease from a saucepan as she answered: 'I don't think that's important, Josy. But as it happens, Mrs Bennett is a very agreeable lady. She usually likes everyone. Now, come along, have you been a naughty girl? Is that why Mrs Bennett's gone home? Or wasn't she feeling well today?'

'Mrs Bennett hasn't been here today—or yesterday,' replied Josy, scooping up a handful of soapsuds and blowing them experimentally. 'Ooh, look! Isn't that pretty——'

'What do you mean, she hasn't been here today or yesterday?' exclaimed Martha incredulously. 'Haven't you been to play school?'

'Not yesterday or today,' affirmed Josy blandly. 'That's why I was playing outside, you see. 'Cos I was so sick of playing indoors.'

Martha didn't understand this. 'But *why* hasn't Mrs Bennett been here? I paid her——'

'She gave Auntie Sarah the money back,' Josy answered, dabbing soapsuds on the end of her nose. 'Do I look funny?'

Martha drew a deep breath. 'Josy, what are you saying?'

'Yes, what are you saying, Josy!' echoed a familiar voice behind them, and Martha swung round to find her sister seated in her wheelchair in the doorway. Sarah's face was unbecomingly flushed, as if she had awoken with a start and rushed to lever herself into her chair, and the pale skin which matched the burnished copper of her hair was blotched and marked with agitation.

'Sarah!' Martha went towards her at once, bending to kiss her sister's cheek, and giving her the benefit of her warm smile. 'How are you? Josy said you were resting. You shouldn't have disturbed yourself. I was going to bring you some tea after I'd finished these dishes.'

'After you'd found out from Josy what had been going on!' countered Sarah testily, lips thin and angry. 'Couldn't you at least have come into my room when you got home? Couldn't you have asked me what had happened, instead of grilling the child?'

Martha was taken aback. 'I wasn't grilling Josy,' she protested. 'But when Mrs Bennett wasn't here ...'

'And has Josy told you why she isn't here?'

'No.' Martha glanced awkwardly at her daughter, wishing she was not witnessing this rather unpleasant scene. 'As a matter of fact, she was just about to do so. But now you can instead.'

Sarah's nostrils flared, and then, as if realising her anger was unjustified, her shoulders slumped. Sitting there, her hands hanging loosely over the arms of her chair, she looked worn and pallid, and painfully thin, and Martha could not sustain her resentment against her. It had not been easy for her sister, acknowledging the extent of her paralysis, and if these last years had been hard for her they had been equally hard for Sarah.

'I found the Bennett woman looking through the drawers of the sideboard,' she explained now, her voice expressionless. 'She said she was looking for a ribbon for Josy's hair. I didn't believe her.'

'She was,' remarked Josy, matter-of-factly, climbing down from the drainer. 'I said that was where you kept them, Mummy, and when I lost my other ribbon on Monday ...'

'Oh, Josy!' Martha stared at her daughter helplessly. Then she turned back to Sarah. 'Didn't Josy tell you?'

'The woman was obviously *not* just looking for ribbons!' declared Sarah, sniffing. 'She had half the contents of the drawer on the sideboard when I caught her. Nosy creature!

She's a horrible woman—I never liked her. She has far too much to say for herself. Just because you pay her to look after Josy, she seems to think she has a right to enter this apartment whenever she likes.'

'Mrs Bennett said that Auntie Sarah was a spiteful old——'

'That will do, Josy!' Martha cut her daughter off with an impatient glance. 'I think the least said about this matter, the better.'

'She had the nerve to throw your money back at me!' persisted Sarah indignantly. 'Can you imagine that? Pound notes fluttering on to the floor!'

'Not very many pound notes,' remarked Martha, realising with a sense of resignation that she would have to go round to Mrs Bennett's after their evening meal and try and straighten things out. She had always found the older woman kind and sympathetic, and if she was inclined to presume on good nature, Martha had made allowances for her.

'Is that all you have to say?' Sarah demanded now. 'Josy and I have had to fend for ourselves these last two days because of that woman's disgraceful behaviour, and all you can say is——'

'Well, let's not get into an argument about it,' suggested Martha rather wearily. 'I'll finish these dishes, then I'll see about making us a meal. After that, we may have some time to talk properly.'

She turned back to the sink as she spoke, so Sarah was more or less obliged to accept this, and Martha heard her asking Josy to go and tidy up her toys in the bedroom. But when they were alone together, her sister could no longer hide her curiosity, and wheeling her chair nearer to the sink, she said:

'Well? What did Myconos say?'

'Myconos?' Martha played for time. '*Aristotle* Myconos?'

'Who else?' Sarah was impatient. 'Don't tell me—he refused, didn't he? You might have known he would.'

Martha lifted the last plate out on to the draining board, and reached for a tea-cloth before replying. Then, starting to dry the knives and forks, she said: 'Yes, he refused. You were right, I shouldn't have gone there.'

'I knew it!' Sarah sat back, triumphant. 'I knew you were wasting your time and your money.'

'Roger's money,' pointed out Martha, dropping cutlery into a drawer. 'You forget, he financed the expedition.'

'Even so ... Going to *that* man! You should have refused.'

Martha sighed. 'Sarah, you forget what Roger has done for us, for *both* of us. Without his help, who knows where we'd be? He lets us this apartment at a nominal rent—he got me that job at the university! Why, he even took us to the Scillies with him last summer, when they were conducting that underwater exploration.'

'Only because you agreed to catalogue the notes for the team,' declared Sarah scornfully. 'You were working till all hours of the day and night. It wasn't much of a holiday for you.'

'No. But Josy had the benefit of the sea and sun,' Martha answered quietly. 'And you looked heaps better when we came back.'

Sarah shrugged. 'It's all very well saying that, but it seems to me, Roger just makes use of you. Why, only last week, he had you transcribing those notes about Santorini——'

'He does pay me,' retorted Martha, finishing drying the dishes and opening the door of the fridge. 'Now, let me see—what do you fancy? Bacon? Eggs? I think there's some fish in the freezer here.'

'No, we had that yesterday,' Sarah contradicted reluctantly. 'It was easy to cook. Roger fried it for us.'

'*Roger!*' Martha almost laughed at her sister's discomfort. 'After all you've said!'

'Well ...' Sarah was indignant, 'someone had to do it. Josy and I couldn't go on eating bread and jam, and when he saw how we were fixed, he offered to make us a meal.'

Martha shook her head. 'You know you could have fried it yourself,' she said, setting a frying pan on the hotplate, and arranging slices of bacon across the base. 'Lots of women in your position have homes and families to care for. And they enjoy proving they're independent.'

Sarah grimaced. 'Don't let's start all that again. I'm doing quite well: I can wash myself and dress myself, and Doctor Sikkim says he's very pleased with my progress.'

'And so am I,' exclaimed Martha sincerely, ashamed of the impatient note in her voice. She was letting other circumstances influence her mood, and it wasn't fair to take her frustration out on her sister.

Nevertheless, aside from the daunting prospect of having to tell Roger she had failed in her mission, she had still the problem of her encounter with Dion to relate. She did not look forward to confiding her mistakes to Sarah, and she did not know how she was going to explain that faltering confession without admitting the methods he had used to gain the information. What he intended to do with his knowledge she dared not contemplate, and she wished she had someone stronger than herself, to whom she could turn in times of trouble.

Roger arrived while they were having their meal. Martha had opened a tin of soup to supplement the bacon and eggs, and he sniffed appreciatively when he put his head round the kitchen door. Tall and angular, with the loose-limbed ungainliness of an excess of height, Roger Scott looked every inch the absent-minded professor. He had straggly red hair above horn-rimmed spectacles, a long nose, and a wide, thick-lipped mouth, and he was one of the cleverest people Martha had ever met. He taught mathematics and economics at the university, and a more unlikely combination would be hard to find for someone steeped in ancient history, and fascinated by any kind of archaeological exploration.

'Hi,' he grinned, levering himself through the opening. 'Something smells good. Hello, Martha. You're back, I see.' He paused, regarding each of them in turn. 'What's wrong? Do I detect a note of despondency about the camp?'

Martha sighed, and then gave him a rueful smile. 'Won't you sit down, Roger? Have some soup. It's chicken, and there's plenty.'

'If you insist.' Roger put down the books he was carrying, and adjusted his long legs under the table. 'Hi, Josy. What a pleasure to see your face clean again. And Sarah! Had any good rows recently?'

'Be quiet, Roger!' exclaimed Sarah irritably, and he transferred his attention to Martha, ladling soup into a bowl.

'Did you open the tin yourself?' he enquired, with wry humour, and she felt her smile appearing again in his uncomplicated company.

'If you don't want it . . .' she challenged, setting the bowl down before him, and he hedged it about with his arm, as if defending all comers. Josy giggled, and even Sarah's features relaxed a little, and Martha resumed her seat, wishing she had some good news to give him. But even had Aristotle been prepared to agree, she doubted he could have done so without Dion's permission, and that was something she would never ask for.

Roger spooned soup into his mouth, and Martha and Sarah exchanged glances. It wasn't fair to keep him in suspense, and pushing her own dish aside, Martha told him she had wasted his money.

'It's no use,' she said, moving her shoulders regretfully.

'The island's sacrosanct. They'll never agree to let anyone excavate there.'

Roger rested his elbows on the table and gave a grunt of resignation. 'Well, it was worth a try,' he remarked, attacking his teeth with a thumbnail. 'You can't be sure of anything until you try, can you, Martha?'

She didn't know why, but that sounded remarkably more than just a rhetorical question. Yet, before she could make any response, he had turned to Josy again, teasing her about her boy-friends missing her at play school, asking Sarah whether she had found the time to read the article about paraplegics he had saved for her. When next he looked at Martha, his eyes were wide and innocent behind the thick lenses, and she wondered if she had mistaken the curiously loaded accent of his comment.

When the meal was over, Sarah offered to supervise Josy's bath while Roger helped her sister with the washing up. Martha thought, rather wryly, that she had hardly had her hands out of water since she arrived home, but she was glad of the opportunity to explain more fully to Roger that she had done her best to help him.

'I'm sure you did,' he agreed, agilely catching the slippery plate that almost fell out of his big hands. 'I guessed it was an unlikely venture, but there was always a chance he might do it for you.'

'For me!' Martha shook her head vigorously. 'I'm *persona non grata* so far as the Myconos family is concerned. You knew that before I went.'

'Did I?' Roger regarded the tea-cloth thoughtfully. 'It occured to me that time might have mellowed old scars. Absence, and all that. Still, it wasn't your husband you went to see, was it? It was his father.'

'Yes.'

The word was clipped, and Roger glanced at her sideways.

'What's up? Don't tell me you saw Dionysus! Is that why you gave me such a funny look at the table, when I made that comment about not being sure of anything?'

'*I*—gave *you* a funny look!' echoed Martha disbelievingly, and Roger nodded.

'Didn't you?'

'No.'

'Oh, well, I thought you did.' Roger shrugged and picked up another plate. 'It was just an idea I had.' He paused. 'So—am I right? Did you see your husband? Or did he resist the temptation to view the heavenly body?'

'Roger!'

'Well!' Roger was unrepentant. 'You do have a heavenly body. Or you would have, if you weren't so damned skinny. So—what happened? Did you realise what you'd been missing all these years?'

'I haven't said Dion was there!'

'But he was, wasn't he? Oh, Martha, your face gives you away every time.'

Martha flushed. 'Well, it wasn't like that anyway.'

'Like what? You realising you'd done the wrong thing by leaving him?'

'Roger, I don't really think this is any of your business!'

'It's not.' He grimaced. 'But you have no one else, do you? Except Sarah. And she's biased enough, as it is.'

'What do you mean?'

Roger sighed, and allowed the plate he had just dried to settle on the rest of the pile. Then, half reluctantly, he said: 'You know.'

'I don't. How could I? I don't even know what you're talking about.'

'Oh, come on ...' Roger pushed his spectacles up his nose, in a curiously boyish gesture. 'You know how Sarah feels about your husband.'

'Oh, that, yes. She never liked him, if that's what you mean. But then Dion never liked her.'

'Which came first, I wonder—the chicken or the egg?'

'What are you talking about?' Martha was growing impatient. 'Roger, I don't really see——'

'Hasn't it ever occurred to you to wonder why Sarah doesn't like your husband?'

'Well—yes.' Martha heaved a deep sigh. 'But I know what you're thinking, and you're wrong. I know that Sarah was attracted to Dion in the beginning, and he turned her off, but that was long before we got married.'

Roger arched his brows. 'Very good. Very shrewd. Very perceptive.'

'Stop mocking me, Roger! Sarah and I don't have any secrets from one another. Sarah's attitude towards Dion is totally concerned with his behaviour towards me! She always said it wouldn't work—my marrying him, and she was right. Rich—and Greek; it was an impossible combination.'

'You think so?' Roger did not sound convinced.

'I know so, don't I?' Martha emptied the dish water away, and began putting the clean dishes away. 'I know you mean well, Roger, but you don't understand.'

Roger shrugged, perching on the corner of the kitchen table. 'Well? Are you going to tell me that you didn't see your husband?'

Martha hesitated. 'No. I saw him.'

'And?'

'Oh, Roger . . .' Martha's nerves were almost at breaking point. 'I'd really rather not talk about it right now. Do you mind? It's been a long day, and I've still to go round and apologise to Mrs Bennett.'

'Mrs Bennett—ah, yes,' Roger nodded. 'Another of Sarah's casualties.'

'What do you mean?'

Roger got off the table. 'I'd better be going. I've got a lecture at nine o'clock in the morning, and I must make some notes. By the way, as this trip to Greece doesn't look like it's coming off, how would you like a few weeks in Ireland instead? They've discovered the wreck of a Spanish galleon off the west coast, and I thought it might make an interesting entry in my book.'

Roger had been writing a book about wrecks and wrecking for the past three years that Martha knew of, but although she doubted it would ever be published, the pleasure it gave him more than made up for the time it consumed.

Now Martha looked at him gratefully, but she shook her head when he urged her to agree. 'You can't take all of us around with you, everywhere you go!' she protested. 'You go and enjoy yourself. I'll type up your notes when you get back.'

'And what will you do for the long weeks of the vacation?' asked Roger with asperity. 'Walk to the park? Take Josy to the zoo? Visit the museum?' He paused. 'Martha, don't worry about the expense. I can afford it. I get a good salary, and my parents didn't exactly leave me penniless. I like doing this for you—and for Sarah, believe it or not. When she's not using that tongue of hers to cut people to pieces, she's quite an intelligent companion. Do you know we've played chess every night since you've been away?'

'I've only been away two nights,' remarked Martha dryly, and Roger's comment that it only seemed like twice that time successfully restored the sense of balance between them.

CHAPTER FOUR

MARTHA did not tell Sarah that night about meeting Dion at Mycos.

Lying in bed later, she chided herself for the coward she was, but her conversation with Roger had convinced her she was not yet ready to face any further advice on the subject. She needed time—time to think, and time to plan, and time to wonder what she would do, if her husband chose to force the issue. She had no illusions that she had heard the last of the affair. Dion was not a man like that. And discussing the matter with Sarah would only cause them both unnecessary pain.

The evening had been taken up, in any case, with placating Mrs Bennett. That lady was much put out at being accused of stealing, and the complaints she had to make about Sarah rang all too true in the face of her sister's admissions.

But Martha succeeded in making her see that without her help, Josy would be obliged to leave her play school, and until she started at the local primary school after the summer holidays, she would be confined to the company of an invalid for the better part of the day.

'Well, I'll continue to take her to school, Mrs Connell,' she said, affording her the married status as a gesture of respect, even though she knew nothing of Martha's background. 'But I won't say I'll get tea for the lassie, if you're to be working late. Not at Meredith Road anyway. I could give her a sandwich here, if you like, when it's necessary, but I won't be accused of interfering again, not when all I've ever tried to do was to be of assistance.'

61

'I understand that, Mrs Bennett.' Martha was only too relieved to hear that Josy was not about to suffer for Sarah's hasty accusations, and she had returned home feeling slightly less distrait than when she had left.

It was a relief to get back to work, and the reassuring surroundings of the university, and during the next couple of days, Martha struggled to catch up on the time she had lost. Most of the students had already left, but the principal, for whom she worked, kept her busy with the paperwork involved in the winding down of the academic year. She was glad of the hectic activity. It kept her mind from other things, and when she walked home from the station on Friday evening, she felt reasonably satisfied with her efforts.

The sight of a foreign-looking green sports car, parked at the kerb outside the house, dispelled her mood abruptly. The residents of Meredith Road did not drive expensive Italian sports cars, and she remembered too well the distinctive lines of a Ferrari to mistake its wide-tyred elegance.

She felt like turning and running, but that would be futile. Besides, Josy was in that house, Josy would be there now, chatting away as she always did, full of the confidence that Martha had instilled in her, probably unaware of the implications of the situation. But Sarah would know, she would be aware, and remembering her sister, Martha broke into a run.

She burst into the living room, gasping for breath, and came to an abrupt halt at the sight of her sister, sitting alone in her chair, a tray of tea on the table beside her. Apart from her sister, the room was empty, and Martha's heart pounded heavily in her chest.

'Where's Josy?' she asked, without giving Sarah a chance to say anything. 'Where is she? I saw a car outside. A Ferrari. I thought—I thought——'

'Yes? What did you think?' Sarah enquired coldly, turn-

ing chilly eyes in her sister's direction. 'That Dion was
here? That he had arrived to take possession of his
daughter?'

Martha's shoulders sagged. 'He *is* here?'

'Not at this moment, no.' Sarah's hands curled and un-
curled about the arms of her chair, revealing her agitation.
'I believe they've gone to the park, though I don't know
which one——'

'You let Dion take Josy ...' Martha began accusingly,
and then broke off as Sarah's balled fist came down hard on
the table.

'Yes,' she said furiously. 'Yes, I *let* him. What else
was I supposed to do? If you don't choose to take me into
your confidence, how am I supposed to defend myself
when—when *that man* comes here, unexpected and unannounced?'

'I wanted to tell you, Sarah,' Martha exclaimed wearily.
'But I needed time ...'

'Well, you've got time now. All the time you need, I
shouldn't wonder. He tells me that you *admitted* that the
child was his. You *admitted* it, Martha. After all you said!'

Martha shifted her weight from one foot to the other,
and then back again, glancing round nervously towards the
door, pacing restlessly across to the screened fireplace.

'You'd better tell me what happened,' she said, trying to
think what she was going to do now that the worst had happened, but Sarah had her own opinions about that.

'I think you ought to tell me how Dion came to learn
about Josy's parentage!' she declared grimly. 'My God!
You must have been *dying* to tell him the truth. You
couldn't wait to spill it, could you? And after everything
that's happened! I don't understand you, Martha, I don't
understand you at all.'

Martha sighed. 'It wasn't like that, Sarah. I didn't just—
tell him.'

'No? What happened? Did he seduce you? Did he spend the nights at the hotel with you? Was it all arranged before you left?'

'No!' Martha felt a rising sense of impatience, which she tried to control. 'You know I never corresponded with Dion. You saw the letters. It was his father I wrote to.'

'Huh!' Sarah sounded unconvinced. 'Are you telling me his father got the information out of you? What did he do? Put you on the rack, or just apply the thumbscrews?'

'Don't be silly, Sarah!'

'What's so silly? If you didn't see Dion——'

'I didn't say I didn't see him.'

'I see. So you did.'

'All right—yes.'

Sarah sighed now. 'You *fool!*'

'Do you think I don't know?' Martha could feel the hot prick of tears behind her eyes. But this was not the time for weeping, and she forced them back. 'Now tell me, where are they? Dion doesn't know London all that well. And that is his car outside, isn't it?'

Sarah shrugged, her expression sullen. 'Josy said she would show him the way,' she admitted.

'Then that means the recreation ground,' declared Martha, checking her flushed cheeks in the mirror. 'I'll go and look for them. How long have they been gone?'

'Not long. Twenty minutes, at the most. Your—husband didn't arrive until after five.'

'After five,' echoed Martha thoughtfully, remembering the wedding. He must have left Athens immediately afterwards.

She moved towards the door, but before she left Sarah exclaimed: 'You're not going to let him take Josy, are you?' and Martha felt the deepening weight of the responsibilities that faced her.

'No,' she said now. 'Not if I can help it. But ...' She

broke off abruptly. 'Does Josy—I mean, did she know who —who Dion was? Did he tell her?'

'Not to my knowledge,' Sarah replied shortly. 'She just took a fancy to him, you know the way she does. And,' more acidly, 'obviously Dion didn't find this place to his liking.'

Martha nodded, and let herself out of the door again. Leaving the house, she took the footpath that led between the houses halfway down Meredith Road, and followed the short cut along the back of the tennis courts to the open expanse of the playing fields.

It was a warm evening, and there were lots of children and their parents around the infants' recreation area. The sand-pit was occupied, and a small queue of toddlers were lined up beside the slide, waiting to climb the iron steps. But Josy was not among them, even though the slide was her favourite piece of apparatus, and Martha looked about her anxiously, wondering if she had mistaken their destination.

She saw Dion suddenly, across the expanse of turf, where an impromptu football match was in progress. He was in the middle of a group of small boys, apparently directing them in the skills of controlling the ball, while Josy stood to one side, holding his coat, apparently well pleased with this unexpected bid for notoriety.

Martha's step faltered before the undoubted popularity of her husband, and the anxiety she had suffered for years over depriving Josy of her father's presence swelled to unmanagable proportions. How could she think that she had compensated for the wealth and security the Myconos' could offer? What could she honestly offer her daughter that Dion could not? Love, perhaps. Possession was not love, as she had learned to her cost, but was that enough? Would Josy have reproached her in years to come if circumstances had not been taken so completely out of her hands?

Dion looked up at that moment and saw her, and her involuntary withdrawal was thwarted. With a word to Josy, he directed her attention towards Martha, and then took his jacket from the child and swung his arms into the sleeves as she came charging across the grass towards her mother. Martha's eyes lingered for a few moments longer on her husband, reluctantly acknowledging his indolent attraction. The narrow pants of his dark suit drew attention to the leanness of his hips, and the matching waistcoat hugged the flat contours of his stomach. His white shirt was quickly concealed as he shrugged into his jacket, but not before she had admired its pristine whiteness. His tailor obviously enjoyed his task, and she was aware of the shortcomings of her own navy linen. But the principal objected to his staff attracting the attention of the students, and in consequence, Martha chose the most unassuming garments for work.

'Mummy, Mummy!' Josy was wrapping her arms excitedly about her mother's hips now. 'Mummy, do you know who's here?'

Martha's mouth was so dry that her tongue clove to its roof, and all she could do was to look down at the child and shake her head in silent denial.

However, Josy didn't seem to notice anything amiss, and gesturing behind her, she exclaimed: 'It's a friend of Daddy's. *My* daddy's,' she added, her eyes shining. 'An old friend. You remember him, don't you, Mummy? Uncle Dion?'

Martha forced herself to lift her head as Dion joined them. Josy's words had reassured her a little, but she was still scarcely competent to meet the challenging glint in her husband's dark eyes.

'Hello, Martha,' he said, with studied politeness. 'I hope you did not object to my taking—Josy for a walk? It was such a beautiful evening, and your—er—sister seemed somewhat—overcome by my appearance.'

Overcome! Martha could imagine Sarah's feelings.

Allowing her tongue to circle her lips, she replied equally politely: 'I don't suppose she ever expected to see you again. You—you should have let us know you were coming.'

Dion's expression hardened. 'But I did,' he declared, his meaning unmistakable. 'Did you not get my message?' Martha stiffened, but before she could make any response, he went on: '*Then pirazi,* I am here now. And I am delighted to make—your daughter's acquaintance.'

'Is Uncle Dion going to stay with us?' demanded Josy, tugging at her mother's skirt, and Martha dragged her eyes away from her husband to concentrate on what the child was saying.

'What? Oh, no—no,' she replied quickly, avoiding Dion's piercing appraisal. 'That is—er—Mr Myconos wouldn't want to stay with us, darling, even if we could accommodate him. He—he has his own apartment.'

'But he said he doesn't live in London!' objected Josy, and Martha expelled her breath impatiently.

'He doesn't. But the—er—the company he works for, they provide somewhere for him to stay, you see.'

Josy's lips pursed. 'Why can't he stay with us?'

'Because we don't have the room!' retorted her mother firmly. 'Now, you run along and play, Josy, while I have a few words with—with Mr Myconos.'

Josy hesitated, looking up at her father. 'You won't go away, will you?' she exclaimed. 'You said you would give me a ride in your car.'

'And I will, I promise,' Dion assured her gently, and Martha wondered how long it had been since he had used that tone to her.

Josy danced off to the play area, and Martha glanced briefly at her husband before starting to walk along the path towards the tennis courts. Dion fell into step beside her, adjusting his long stride to her shorter one, and she thought how innocent their companionship must seem to other people, how uncomplicated the relationship that was presently causing her such turmoil. It was years since she and Dion had walked together, years since she had sensed the envy of other women, and felt herself so fortunate to be part of his life.

The silence between them lengthened, but eventually he spoke. 'She is very like you, is she not?' he remarked without emotion. 'I like her. You have done well.'

Martha said nothing, trying to marshall her defences, and he went on: 'Why are you so afraid of me, Martha? What have I ever done to make you fear me?'

Martha expelled her breath in a gasp, turning to face him with trembling dignity. 'What do you intend to do, Dion?' she demanded, taking the initiative. 'Why have you really come here? What manner of action is your vengeance going to take, because I don't believe you just came here to—to *meet* Josy.'

A trace of ironic humour deepened the lines beside his eyes, as he surveyed her uneasy defiance, and with a mocking finger he reached out and touched the compressed outline of her mouth. She flinched away from him, pressing the back of one hand to her lips, and his shoulders moved in mild impatience as he said:

'Why did you lie to me, Martha? Why did you let me go on believing the child was not mine, when it is obvious, even to the least discerning of intelligences, that she is?'

Martha held up her head. 'I *never* lied to you, Dion. I never once said the child was not yours.'

'No,' he agreed swiftly, unable to control the sudden burst of anger that gripped him. 'But you did not deny that it was not anyone else's either!'

Martha gulped. 'And you think I should have done that?' she demanded unsteadily. 'You really think I ought to have attempted to convince you of my innocence?'

'It would not seem unreasonable——'

'Would it not?' Martha found strength in her own anger. My God, Dion! What do you think I am? What manner of husband expects his wife to assure him that the child she's just given birth to is *his*?'

'*Hristo*, it was not like that, and you know it!' Dion's dark features contorted violently. 'Any other wife——'

'Any other *Greek* wife, you mean!'

'No.' Dion gripped the back of his neck with convulsive fingers. 'You know how things were between us before the child was born!'

'Do I not?'

'Then you must realise how I was feeling——'

'How you were feeling?' Martha snorted, and Dion released his neck to grasp her forearm.

'Yes. How I was feeling,' he agreed grimly. 'I do have feelings, you know, despite what you think of me!'

Martha looked down at his fingers on her arm. 'Oh, I know you have feelings,' she got out chokingly. 'Feelings of suspicion and jealousy——'

'And *love*!' he grated forcefully. 'Or I had, before you did your level best to destroy it!'

'Love!' Martha's lips curled. 'You don't know the meaning of the word.'

Dion looked as if he would have liked to have done her some physical injury. But the park was too public a place to indulge in histrionics of that sort, and with a stifled oath he released her, thrusting his hands into the pockets of his pants and turning aside from her.

Martha rubbed her arm, and followed his gaze to where Josy was climbing the steps to the top of the slide. Was it only a mother's pride, or did she really stand out from the other children? Certainly, she was an attractive little girl, with her fair skin and exotically dark hair. Nature had blended her colouring with Dion's to produce an unusual mixture, and in a few years Josy would be an outstandingly beautiful young woman. Was it fair to expect Dion to sacrifice his share in that awakening, whatever their personal differences might be? Other families came to an amicable arrangement. Why shouldn't they? There was no point to these senseless recriminations. They were all in the past, and no matter how he had learned of his daughter's existence, he knew now, and there was no way of altering it.

'I—I suppose you intend to tell her,' Martha said now, trying to speak calmly. 'Josy, I mean. You do intend to tell her you're her father, don't you?'

For a moment, Dion did not answer her, but then he turned towards her again, and now there was cold decision where only moments before, looking on his daughter, there had been tender admiration.

'I want her, Martha,' he said, his words striking her straight to the heart. 'And I intend to get her, one way or the other.'

Martha had to grasp the metal fencing of the tennis courts for support as she echoed faintly: 'You want her? What do you mean—you want her? I'm prepared to come to some reasonable arrangement with you concerning rights of access, but——'

'Not rights of access, Martha.' He was inflexible. 'I mean I intend to take her back to Greece. To live with me, as *my* daughter should.'

Martha trembled. 'You can't do that!'

'Why can I not?' His lips curled. 'Do you think any court in either my country or yours would deny that I can do far more for her than you ever could?'

'Money's not everything——'

'As you persist in telling me. But I suggest that it does buy me a certain amount of advantage, not least in the legal field. And in the circumstances, it would seem you have— too many responsibilities as it is.'

Martha's face drained of colour. 'You—you wouldn't,' she protested weakly. 'You wouldn't use Sarah's incapacitation as a lever!'

'Why not?' Dion regarded her without sympathy. 'Do I
not have the right to use any methods to gain my own
ends? You created this situation, Martha. You took my
daughter away from me. Why should I care if you find you
have taken more upon yourself that you can successfully
cope with?'

Martha pressed her quivering lips together. 'But—but
that's inhuman!'

'And was it humane to treat me as you did?' he snapped.
'How do you think I felt? Deprived of my wife and my
child in one crushing blow! I could have killed you then,
Martha. I wanted to, believe me! But I allowed myself to be
—persuaded. Instead of pursuing my instincts and following you to London, I used the company as a palliative until
I had myself in control again. You can thank my family for
that.' He moved his shoulders in a dismissing gesture. 'Of
course, by the time I did come to find you, my solicitors
told me you had moved, to this house in Wimbledon owned
by your *family* friend, Roger Scott!'

Martha passed a hand over her eyes. 'We had to move.
Sarah was the victim of a hit-and-run driver. The flat—
her flat—the one she rented after we got married and the
house was sold, was no use to her in a wheelchair. Besides,
with the baby ...'

'But you did not choose to inform me of that, did you?'
Dion demanded cuttingly. 'In fact, *you* did not even answer
my letters.'

'There was nothing to say.' Martha sighed, moving her
shoulders in a helpless gesture. 'I wanted nothing from
you.'

'And now?' he countered, forcing her to look up at him,
and she felt the impotence of her position in the face of
his authority.

'Why can't you leave us alone?' she exclaimed, appealing to him unwillingly. 'You said I'd done a good job of

bringing Josy up. Why can't I go on doing so? We could come to some arrangement ...'

Dion regarded her without expression. 'What arrangement?' he asked flatly. 'That she lives with you and spends holidays with me?'

Martha's hopes rekindled. 'That's a possibility.'

'No.' Dion shook his head.

'No?'

'No.' He looked down at his booted feet. 'That would not suit me at all. I want my daughter with me!'

Martha gulped. 'She's a person in her own right, you know,' she protested. 'You can't just take her from me!'

'Do not imagine I could not persuade her,' retorted Dion coldly. 'I am her father, and there is something of me in her, despite her likeness to you. A child can be won in so many ways—with toys, with the promise of luxuries, with the exciting prospect of changed surroundings. *And with love!*' he added, before she could interrupt. 'I have grandparents to offer her, aunts and uncles, cousins, she does not even know exist! Quite confusing for so small a girl, no?'

One word in all he had said stuck in Martha's consciousness. '*Could?*' she whispered faintly. 'You said—you *could* persuade her. What does that mean? Don't you intend to?'

Dion studied her troubled face for several seconds, his eyes intent and probing, then he looked again towards the playing area, where Josy was sampling the delights of the sand-pit. While Martha strove to contain her anxiety, he watched the antics of his daughter as she shovelled sand into her bucket, his mouth softening with indulgence when she produced a crumbling sand-castle.

However, when he turned back to Martha again the indulgence had disappeared, and she waited apprehensively for his answer. 'No,' he said at last, when her nerves were stretched to breaking point. 'No, I do not intend to take her from you. In spite of your selfishness, I could not do that.'

He paused. 'What I do intend to do is take you back again——'

'No——'

'—and as Sarah obviously depends on you so heavily, I am prepared to offer her a home as well!'

CHAPTER FIVE

MARTHA'S head swam. She had had little enough to eat that day, just a slice of toast and some coffee for breakfast, a cup of soup at her desk at lunchtime, and it was already after the time they normally ate their evening meal. Even so, the nauseating giddiness that gripped her was far from just lightheadedness, and noticing her ashen features, Dion took sympathy on her at last.

'Come,' he said, almost gently. 'I will get Josy, and we will go back to the house and collect the car. Then we will have dinner together. We need to talk. There are plans to be made, arrangements——'

'No!' Martha managed to voice the word with difficulty. 'Dion, no! I can't—I *won't* go back to Greece!'

His expression hardened instantly. 'I think you do not have much choice in the matter,' he asserted coldly. 'Unless you intend to run away from me again, and I assure you, if you should do so, you would not get away so easily this time.'

'Oh, Dion ...'

She closed her eyes against the implacability of his expression, and heard him call their daughter. Josy came at once, eager to take his hand and skip along beside him, completely trusting his averred connection with her father, unaware of her mother's emotional trauma.

The walk back to Meredith Road seemed endless to Martha. She had never felt so lost or so alone, and Josy's excited chatter only served to underline the gulf Dion was capable of opening between them. She felt dazed and bewildered, unable to comprehend his plans for her—or his motives—and she could only assume his reasons for taking her back encompassed a desire to make her suffer for the humiliation he must have experienced when she left him. Of a certainty, he did not care for her. His attitude towards her made that patently clear, and as he must know how she felt about him what possible satisfaction could he get out of it? His indifference towards her feelings—her work, and the life she had made for herself—was denigrating, his arrogance overwhelming. He didn't trouble himself with insignificant details. In his world, the Myconos word was law.

She contemplated the alternatives. If she refused to go back to him he would find some way to take Josy from her. One read in the papers every day of tug-of-love children, torn between their parents, snatched from their homes and never seen again. Dion would not even have to do that. As he said, what could she offer the child? Would the circumstances in which they lived be considered suitable by any court of law? Might the fact that she had to go out to work every day influence their decision against her? Could she take the risk that it might not?

She knew she couldn't, although the prospect of relating Dion's ultimatum to Sarah filled her with despair. Sarah had taken an almost pathological dislike towards her husband, and she would not take kindly to the idea of leaving London. Where would they live? Dion had not discussed that with her. Mycos or Athens, did it really matter? She was caught in a trap of her own making.

When they reached the house in Meredith Road, Dion paused beside his car, propping himself against the hood before saying: 'Collect your coats, or whatever else you need. I will wait here, while you tell your sister the good news.'

'No.' Martha determined not to be coerced into obeying him completely. He couldn't *make* her have dinner with him. And ignoring Josy's disappointed face, she said: 'I can't go with you. Sarah is waiting for her evening meal. Whether you like it or not, I won't neglect my responsibilities.'

Dion straightened, the shrewd eyes narrowed between silky dark lashes. '*Poli kala*,' he averred, giving his daughter's shoulder a squeeze. 'I will have dinner here. Does that please you, little one?'

Josy pursed her lips. 'You said you would take me for a ride!' she protested, and Dion inclined his head.

'So I will. Right this moment.' He looked at Martha, his eyes cool and inscrutable. 'Five minutes only?' he suggested, and she moved her shoulders helplessly.

'Can I stop you?' she muttered, in an undertone, and without waiting for his response she brushed past them, up the path and into the house.

Roger was with Sarah when she came into the living room, and he gave her a sympathetic smile. 'I hear you've got a visitor,' he commented, getting up from the armchair by the fireplace. 'I guess I'm to blame for that.'

Martha shook her head. 'No. I am,' she declared, running a bemused hand over her hair, reassured to find that the chignon she wore for work was still in place. 'We've got a visitor for supper, too, as it happens, so will you excuse me while I see what I can offer him?'

'Dion!' Sarah burst out angrily. 'Dionysus Myconos is eating with us?'

'Who else?' said Martha wearily, pausing in the kitchen doorway. 'Sarah, please, don't cause problems. I've got enough of them as it is.'

Roger moved awkwardly towards the door. 'I guess I'd better be going,' he remarked, but Martha came back into the room as he spoke and put out a detaining hand.

'No, don't go, Roger,' she exclaimed appealingly. 'I mean, won't you stay and eat with us, too? I—er—I'd be glad of your support.'

'His support?' echoed Sarah, wheeling her chair towards

them. 'Martha, what's going on? Why do you need Roger's support? What has that man been saying to you?'

'Roger, please——' Martha appealed to him again, and he moved his shoulders in an offhand gesture.

'Well, if you really want me to stay ...'

'I do,' said Martha, disappearing into the kitchen again, and Sarah wheeled her chair after her with a frown of concentration creasing her brow.

'Martha!' she insisted. 'If you don't tell me what's going on, I shall go to my room and stay there. I may do that in any case. I have no desire to sit at table with that man!'

Martha paused in the process of taking some frozen steaks out of the fridge, and after a moment's hesitation, she said: 'He wants Josy, Sarah. He says he'll take me to court for custody if—if——'

'If what?'

'—if I don't agree to—to go back to him.'

'*What?*' Sarah was obviously as stunned as Martha had been.

'It's true. He—he says he's prepared to take us both—well, all three of us, actually—for—for Josy's sake, I suppose.'

Sarah stared at her as if she couldn't believe her ears. 'You can't be serious!'

'I am.' Martha could not sustain her sister's accusing stare, and she turned away to peel the plastic from the meat. 'I know it isn't easy to accept, but—well, he didn't actually give me much choice.'

'You mean you've *agreed*!'

Martha bent her head. 'I haven't—disagreed,' she amended. 'Oh, I refused at first, of course, but when—when the situation was made clear to me ...'

'You can't do it, Martha!'

Martha sighed. 'What else can I do?'

'You can fight him, of course.'

'And if I lose?'

'You're losing without even trying.'

'I'm trying to be fair to Josy,' declared Martha defensively. 'It—it's been on my mind for some time ...'

'What? Going back to him? Is that why you told him——'

'No, no, no!' Martha put her palms over her ears, as if to silence the doubts that were plaguing her as well as her sister. 'Sarah, try to understand! If I do as you say—if I go to court—I may never see Josy again.'

'Rubbish! They couldn't deny you access.'

'Access! Access!' Martha stared at her. 'Do you think that's all I want—*access*? Sarah, Josy's my daughter, the only child I'm ever likely to have. I can't give her up. *I can't*!'

'You may marry again,' said Sarah impatiently. 'You're young. You have your health.' There was bitterness in her tone now. 'If you were crippled, you could state that with certainty, but you can't. Why, you could meet some other man tomorrow ...'

'No, Sarah.' Martha turned back to the steaks again, and with an angry oath her sister wheeled her chair about.

'So I'm not even to be consulted,' she said coldly. 'Well, don't expect me to accompany you, because I won't.'

'Sarah!' Martha's face mirrored her dismay, but her sister was adamant.

'I mean it. I have no intention of giving that man any power over me! You can go, if you like. Leave me—I'll manage somehow. But I shan't go with you, so don't imagine I'll change my mind.'

'Sarah!'

But the wheelchair had already disappeared into the living room, and with a sinking heart Martha forced herself to concentrate on cooking the food.

In spite of her lack of enthusiasm, the steaks were soon grilling to perfection, and the salad she had prepared to go with them was crisp and light. Fortunately she had bought some cheese the day before, and that accompanied by crackers would have to do as a dessert. Nevertheless, the food was the least of her worries, and as the minutes since Dion and Josy had left stretched from ten to fifteen, and from fifteen to twenty, she felt the stirring fear of wondering whether he intended to bring her back.

Roger, who must have overheard her argument with her sister, was a tower of strength. Ignoring Sarah's resentful silence, he began to talk about a film they had all seen on the television the night before, asking if Martha had read the book, and whether she agreed that the plot had been simplified to appeal to a larger audience. It was always easier to explain complicated situations in a book, he asserted, when the author was able to use the character's thoughts as an explanation for his activities.

Martha tried to answer him, but her mind wasn't really capable of summoning an opinion, and she was searching for an apology when she heard the crunch of tyres in the road, and the smooth braking of an engine.

'They're back,' remarked Roger, his eyes gentle with understanding. 'Now you can breathe again.'

Martha hesitated only a moment, and then hastened into the kitchen to check on the steaks. Sarah looked at Roger, then wheeled her chair towards the door, but he stepped into her path.

'You must stay and greet your brother-in-law,' Martha heard him say rather sardonically, and Sarah's angry remonstrance went unheard beneath the boisterous excitement of Josy's entrance.

Martha came to the door of the kitchen reluctantly, and Josy immediately made a beeline for her. 'It's super!' she cried, gazing up at her mother with sparkling eyes. 'Uncle Dion's car, I mean. It goes ever so fast! But he didn't drive too fast, because if you do, a policeman might stop you from driving altogether.'

'I'm glad you enjoyed it, darling,' Martha managed,

with a tight smile, and lifted her head as Dion followed his daughter into the room.

His eyes went straight to her, then to Roger, and finally to Sarah. Closing the door behind him, he offered a slight bow of his head in her sister's direction, then looked questioningly at the other man.

'Oh—er—this is Roger Scott, Dion.' Martha stumbled over her words in her haste. 'Roger, this is—this is Dion Myconos.'

'Hello.' Roger shook the other man's hand politely, and they weighed one another up in silent appraisal. Sarah said nothing, hands folded in her lap, eyes downcast, and with a feeling of escape Martha turned back into the kitchen.

The steaks were cooked, and she looked about her doubtfully. The kitchen was quite large, large enough for the three of them to eat at any rate, and four on occasion. But five? And Dion? Martha shook her head. She would have to think again.

'I brought you this.' Dion's voice behind her brought her head round with a jerk, and she turned it to find her husband offering her a bottle, wrapped in tissue paper. 'That was what took us so long. I could not find a suitable dealer. It is just a small contribution, that is all.'

'Well—thank you.' Martha unwrapped the paper and examined the label. It was a favourite of hers from years past, a rich claret, that would complement the meal ideally.

'We eat in here?' enquired Dion, not leaving as she had hoped, but glancing about him curiously. 'There is not a lot of room, but no doubt we can manage.'

'I—er—I thought we might eat in the living room,' murmured Martha uncomfortably, eyeing Dion's dark suit. 'I mean—oh, God!' Her voice dropped to an undertone. 'You *know* what I mean.'

'You think I am too proud to eat in the kitchen?' he suggested crisply, eyebrows arched in interrogation. 'When did I ever give you that impression? As I recall it, you have cooked for me on other occasions. At the house in Maxwell Grove, for example!'

Martha opened a drawer and took out a tablecloth, spreading it on the table without another word. His mention of her parents' house had been deliberate, she was sure, recalling as it did the early days of their relationship, before the bonds of being Dion's wife had tightened the threads about her. They had been so happy in those days, so eager and in love—or she had been in love, she amended, remembering the jealousy that had stifled all other emotion.

Before they were married, they had spent a lot of time at Maxwell Grove. It was somewhere they could be together, could be alone, if Sarah was out, and Martha had wanted to be alone with Dion at that time, more than anything else. It held other memories, too, memories of the first time he had made love to her, and the soaring ecstasy she had experienced when he taught her the delights of physical possession.

Possession, she thought bitterly now. Why did everything always come back to that word? In those days, it had been something to cherish, not to challenge.

Dion had removed his jacket now, draping it over the back of one of the chairs, loosening the top button of his shirt beneath the dark tie. The scent of his body drifted across to her, warm after the heat of the day, and she was glad when Josy's childish tones interrupted them, and she could thrust her unwanted memories away.

'Roger's staying for supper, too,' she announced to no one in particular. 'Auntie Sarah's just told me. But she says to tell you she doesn't want any supper.'

Martha's lips tightened. 'She will, when she sees it,' she replied, with more confidence than she felt. 'Josy, get the glasses out of the sideboard, will you? The ones with the stems. And tell Auntie Sarah that she's got to eat something because I've made it for her.'

'Your sister does not forget,' remarked Dion dryly,

glancing about him thoughtfully. 'Where is a corkscrew? So I can open the wine.'

'Sarah says she won't leave England,' declared Martha tautly, rummaging through the cutlery drawer. 'I can't go and leave her alone.'

Dion's impatience exhibited itself in the way he pushed her aside and located the implement for himself. Inserting the pointed screw, he uncorked the bottle expertly, and then rather harshly he demanded:

'When are you going to realise you are not your sister's keeper, and she is not yours? Of course she says she will not leave England, because she knows how guilty that will make you feel. *Etsi*, you tell her you are leaving. Then we will see what she will decide.'

Martha gave him a resentful look. 'You feel no remorse, do you, Dion? Sarah's accident means nothing to you.'

He shrugged. 'I know if our positions were reversed, she would spit on me. Why should I pity her? She has always tried to come between us. She is doing it still.'

'There is nothing between us, Dion!' Martha choked hotly. 'Don't imagine because you appear to hold all the cards that I have no will of my own! I'm not a puppet, Dion. I don't jump when I'm told. And if you think by forcing me to come back to you, I shall change my opinion of you, you're very much mistaken!'

He moved his shoulders in a dismissing gesture, but he did not make any response, and Josy's return with the glasses prevented any pursuance of that particular exchange. 'Auntie Sarah says she isn't hungry,' she remarked, putting the glasses down on the table. 'I think she means it, Mummy, because she got quite angry when I said what you told me to say.'

Dion's eyes flickered, and patting her head he said: 'Do not worry about your aunt, little one. She will change her mind, never fear.' But he was looking at Martha when he said it.

Martha served the meal on to plates before putting it on the table. There was not enough room for serving dishes as well as everything else, and the table looked quite attractive once the wine was poured.

'Will you come through, Roger?' she asked, going to the door of the living room, and he nodded goodnaturedly, propelling Sarah's chair before him in spite of her protests.

'You can't absent yourself from the family gathering,' he assured her mockingly, pushing her chair to the table. 'Mmm, this looks delicious, Martha. I only wish I had someone to cook for me every night.'

Dion cast the other man a thoughtful glance as they sat down, and presently he asked: 'You consider yourself a part of this family—er—Scott? My wi—that is, *Martha*—told me you are—what would you say?—the family friend, no?'

'That's right,' Roger nodded. 'Our parents were friends years ago. And when Martha and Sarah needed somewhere else to live, I was happy to offer them this place.' He grimaced. 'It's not much, I know, but it's cheap.'

'We'd have been lost without you, Roger,' Martha assured him indignantly, uncaring what Dion thought, and she was surprised when her husband seconded her gratitude.

'I can see I have much to thank you for,' he observed quietly, his eyes resting on Josy as she sawed rather clumsily at the meat. Then his eyes shifted to Sarah as he went on: 'I regret we did not meet earlier.'

Roger's eyes met Martha's across the width of the table, but he didn't make any comment, and she was grateful. Instead, he swallowed a mouthful of his wine before complimenting her on the tenderness of the steak, and she hoped her husband would take the hint and not turn the meal into an interrogation.

Sarah had listened to this interchange without comment. The sight and the smell of the meal had proved too much for her, and she, like everyone else, was enjoying the food, although her eyes strayed often in her sister's direction, and there was bitterness as well as resentment in her stare.

Martha, for her part, found the food nauseating. In spite of the emptiness of her stomach, her throat refused to open, and she chewed the meat over and over again until the wine forced a passage down to her stomach.

'I understand you have an interest in antiquity, Scott.' Dion spoke again, and Martha glanced apprehensively at her other guest.

'That's right,' Roger agreed amicably. 'It's my hobby. I've always enjoyed poking about old ruins.' He grinned at the girl in the wheelchair beside him. 'That's why Sarah and I get along so well.'

'Your appalling humour is only superseded by your manners!' she retorted irritably, giving him a venomous look, and Martha cleared her throat to disguise the hysterical gulp that threatened to escape her. It was typical of Roger to tease her sister in this way, but the implications were so serious, she felt nearer to tears than laughter.

Dion rescued the situation by asking Roger about his research into ancient Greece. 'I believe you have a particular interest in the eruption on Thera,' he remarked, using the old name for Santorini. 'Have you ever been there?'

Roger shook his head. 'Unfortunately not.' He paused. 'Have you?'

Martha was surprised when her husband nodded. 'Once,' he agreed evenly. 'It is not an attractive place. One sails into the gulf surrounded by gaunt cliffs, and despite their colouring, they have no charm. Of course, you know the story of how the volcano erupted and the middle of the island sank and the sea poured in, only to be spewed out again in the tremendous tidal wave that engulfed Crete more than seventy miles away. That kind of catastrophe leaves a certain—atmosphere, no? Oh, there are villages and people, and life goes on. But somehow the mules that carry one from the harbour to the capital, Fira, and which are supposed to contain the souls of the dead, seem to epitomise the tragedy in terms of what was lost, you understand?'

Roger had been listening intently, and now he broke in to ask whether Dion had seen the two blocks of lava which had appeared in the crater where the volcano used to stand.

'Nea Kameni and Palea Kameni?' Dion inclined his head. 'The "Old Burnt Island" and the "New Burnt Island",' he quoted. 'Yes, of course. Have you heard them described as being reminiscent of the surface of the moon? They are like sentinels to the cataclysm, and when one observes a shred of smoke rising from them, one cannot help but feel aware of one's own mortality.'

'I didn't know you were interested in archaeology,' Roger said now, avoiding the awkward position of not knowing how to address Dion. 'Have you made any studies on Mycos itself?'

Dion smiled then, and Martha wondered if Roger was aware of how deceptive a smile could be. 'One does not need to be interested in archaeology to know the legend of Thera,' he replied smoothly. 'You forget, Greece is my home. The islands are an integral part of my life, and I too find their history fascinating.'

'But Santorini has baffled historians for years,' exclaimed Roger eagerly. 'There's still speculation about Solon's theory of Atlantis, and your own Professor Marinatos claimed that perhaps Solon's confusion over the dates was nothing more than a clerical error.'

'I can see you find it fascinating, too,' remarked Dion dryly. 'You know of course that the abscence of any human remains beyond a few bones and some charred teeth points to the suggestion that the inhabitants had time to flee before disaster struck. There are comparisons with Pompeii to be made, although it is doubtful that any craft could have withstood the tidal wave that followed on the eruption.'

'That's my whole theory,' Roger explained, resting his elbows on the table and leaning forward enthusiastically. 'If there were any survivors, Mycos might have given them refuge.'

'Oh, honestly, must we spend the whole meal talking about some extinct civilisation!' Sarah protested irritably. 'We all know of your preoccupation with the past, Roger, but for myself, I would rather know what is going to happen in the present.' She looked challengingly towards her sister. 'Are you leaving, Martha? I think I have a right to be told. Or am I expected to find out about that as well as everything else?'

'Leaving?' It was Josy who took up her aunt's words, her childish features revealing an anxious bewilderment. 'Where are you going, Mummy? You didn't tell me——'

Martha cast a frustrated glance at Sarah, as she strove to reassure her daughter. 'Nothing's been decided yet, poppet,' she replied firmly. 'Auntie Sarah is just talking about something that—might happen, that's all.'

Dion's fingers circled his wine glass. 'What your mother is trying to say, Josy, is that I have—suggested to her that you all might like to come and live in my country, with me.'

Josy's eyes widened. 'In your country?'

'Greece,' agreed Dion quietly. 'Your—father's country.'

'Why don't you tell her, Dion?' demanded Sarah scornfully, and Martha's lips parted in dismay at her words. 'You want to, so why don't you? Or aren't you prepared to commit yourself that far?'

'Sarah ...'

Roger's rueful admonishment was a mild reproof, but Dion's warning was unmistakable. 'Do not try to fence with me, Sarah,' he advised. 'We know one another too well to indulge in that kind of foolishness. You would be advised to hold your tongue on occasions when your opinion is not invited, unless you wish me to explain certain—how shall I say?—inconsistencies in your attitude, to my wife.'

Martha's eyes went automatically to Josy at this admission, but the little girl hadn't noticed his lapse, or if she had, she did not associate it with her mother. Instead, she was sitting looking rather pensive, and Martha guessed she was still mulling over his earlier statement. This apartment, such as it was, had always spelled security to Josy, and she was too young to worry about anything else.

At least his words had shocked Sarah into silence, and she was staring moodily down at her plate. The atmosphere around the table had thickened with their individual tension, and although Martha knew her sister was really to blame, she couldn't help acknowledging that without Dion's presence, the situation would never have arisen.

This time it was Josy who retrieved a sense of normality, saying curiously: 'Where do you live, Uncle Dion? Do you have a house like Roger? Or just an apartment like us?'

Dion's hard features softened. It was amazing how indulgent he could be when it suited his purpose, Martha thought rather maliciously, realising that Josy was enjoying her unexpected popularity.

'I have several houses—and an apartment,' her father admitted after a moment. 'But houses do not mean a lot. It is the—the people who live in them who matter.'

Martha's knuckles clenched about her knife and fork, and she had to bite her tongue not to respond to that particular piece of propaganda. Those had been her words to Dion, during one of their frequently heated arguments, and he was deliberately using them against her now.

'Several houses ...' Josy sounded impressed, her eyes wide with wonder, the rest of her salad neglected on her plate. 'That's more than one, isn't it? Do you live in all of them?'

'Your—er—*Uncle* Dion is a wealthy man, Josy,' Martha

interposed shortly, resenting his influence. 'He can afford to buy anything he likes.'

'Including people,' remarked Sarah almost inaudibly, pushing her chair away from the table. 'If you'll excuse me . . .'

'We do not.' Dion rose to his feet as Sarah would have left them, and she glanced back at him resentfully, aware like Martha of his overpowering arrogance. 'Before you leave us, Sarah, I want you to know that I intend to get my own way in this.'

'Don't you always?' she countered bitterly, and he essayed a polite bow in her direction.

'As you say,' he agreed, acknowledging the irony. 'But I should also like your compliance with my arrangements.'

Sarah's lips worked silently for a few moments, then she said: 'You can't force me to come with you, Dion. Whatever you threaten.'

Dion's eyes narrowed. 'I do not intend to threaten you, Sarah. I merely wish to make it clear that Martha owes her allegiance to me first—and you second. Do you understand?'

Sarah sniffed. 'That sounds remarkably like a threat to me,' she exclaimed.

'Sarah!' It was Roger who spoke now, but she jerked away from his restraining hand, and Dion shrugged his shoulders rather wearily.

'It is your decision, of course,' he said, meeting Martha's frustrated gaze, and then, as if suddenly having an idea, he added: 'I have been thinking. Perhaps I could persuade my father to allow—Scott access to the island. Providing he is alone, I see no reason why that might not be arranged.' He ignored Roger's excited exclamation, and went on: 'It might be convenient for all of us to spend some time at the villa.'

Martha dragged her eyes away from his, her heart pounding heavily in her ears. Oh, he was clever, she thought bitterly, very clever! By inviting Roger to Mycos, he was destroying Sarah's one chance of remaining alone in London. Without Roger's help she could never look after herself, and gradually he was eroding any opposition she might make to his plans.

Sarah was looking at her across the table, and Martha could see that the same thought had occurred to her. But Sarah was not his wife, and she still retained some thread of independence.

'I know what you're trying to do, Dion,' she declared, tremulously, her hands clutching and unclutching the arms of her chair. 'You think if Roger leaves, too, I'll be forced to do the same!'

'And will you not?' asked Dion quietly, while Josy stared from one to the other of them, scarcely comprehending the half of this.

'No.' Sarah swallowed convulsively. 'I—I—there's a woman who looks after Josy sometimes—Mrs Bennett. I—I'll get her to come in when I need her.'

'Oh, Sarah ...' began Martha helplessly, but Josy was not so tactful.

'Mrs Bennett won't come if Mummy's not here,' she exclaimed innocently. 'You know what she said——'

'That will do, Josy!'

Martha started to correct her, but Dion still had the last word. 'What if I say—your Mr Scott's permission hinges on your accepting the arrangements, Sarah?' he ventured softly, bringing a groan of protest from Roger. 'Can you deny him this opportunity, after all he has done for you?'

And Martha knew that Sarah could not.

CHAPTER SIX

MARTHA listened to the sound of childish laughter coming from the direction of the swimming pool, and shifted rather restlessly on the cushioned lounger. It was amazing how easily her daughter had adapted to this change in her surroundings, and Martha assumed, somewhat ruefully, that she must be more like her father than she had thought. Josy had taken to the life at the villa like a duck to water, and in addition, despite the fairness of her skin, she was already losing that delicate pallor.

They owed a lot to Alex, of course, Martha reflected, hearing his teasing banter over the splashing sound of the water. Without his companionship, these first few days on Mycos would have been empty indeed, and his patience with Josy seemed never-ending. Whether he had guessed the child's true identity, she could not be sure, for they did not discuss it. But at least their relationship had improved since he had learned of Dion's intentions of taking her back again, although again it was not something they actually discussed. In the evenings, when Roger returned from his day's exploration at Simos, at the north end of the island, and they all joined together for dinner here on the patio, conversation was always impersonal, and she herself had postponed precipitating explanations until she felt more capable of handling them.

Of course, had Dion been there it would have been different. But she ought to have realised that his schedule would not allow him more than a perfunctory interest in their establishment, and apart from a phone call the day after their arrival, they had had no word from him.

In one way, she had been relieved. It had enabled her to get her bearings without the constant anxiety of wondering exactly what he might demand of her. Even so, there were times when she could have wished that obstacle might be faced, and she couldn't prevent the weakening rush of blood that accompanied such anticipation. If only the flesh was as controllable as the mind, she thought, and then chided herself for being such a fool. She had to remember that this was the man who had doubted his own child's paternity, and who had been prepared to believe that she had lied to him all along. How had things got so bad between them that such a conversation should ever take place?

Her visits to London had not helped. Indeed, they had been the seed from which Dion's core of suspicion had grown. But how could he expect her to abandon Sarah after they were married, knowing as he did that until Martha's marriage they had been so close? Sarah had expected her to visit, and because she had refused to come to Greece, Martha had been obliged to make the trip to England. She had thought she understood Sarah's feelings about seeing Dion. After all, she had been so attracted to him in the beginning, and his preference for her sister must have been hard to bear. But Sarah's dislike of her husband had hardened into something more than mere resentment, and when things began to turn sour for Martha, Sarah had always been there to reassure her.

It would be easy, she thought, to attribute some of the blame to Sarah's attitude. Easy to make Sarah the scapegoat for what had, ultimately, become an impossible situation. But if it had not been Sarah, it would likely have been someone else, some other excuse for Dion to exhibit his almost pathological jealousy. He had bought her, she thought bitterly, and he thought he owned her, that she should have no will outside that which he decreed. And because she had become pregnant, at a time when she had stated that they ought to wait a few more years, he had immediately suspected the worst.

Martha stretched her arms above her head, noticing as she did so that her skin, too, was turning a becoming shade of honey. She had been quite brown when she lived with Dion, and the blending of her skin and hair tones had always enchanted him. He was so dark, the hairs on his arms and legs so great a contrast to hers.

A curious pain twisted inside her. Had it never occurred to him to contemplate the circumstances of Josy's conception? In the heat of his anger, had he never speculated that he might have been responsible? Had he forgotten so quickly that weekend they had spent at Delphi? That fleeting weekend they had snatched from his hectic schedules, in an attempt to recapture the relationship they had shared before work, and their families, came between them.

Martha had wanted to visit the temple of Apollo, and Dion had agreed to indulge her. They had driven up in the late afternoon, when the air was soft and muted by mountain shadow, and the slopes below Parnassus seemed to quiver with the expectancy of myth and legend. Any moment one might see the goat-like Pan, and his horned satyrs, or glimpse the muses in their sacred groves, and Delphi itself rose from antiquity, like 'the navel of the earth' which was what the ancients had called it.

Their hotel had been small and intimate, the manager an associate of Dion's, and quite prepared to offer them the very best of his hospitality. And they had done what the other tourists had done, and visited the Temple of Apollo, and the sanctuary of Apollo, and the Kastalian spring. They had even wandered round the museum, and dined on the terrace overlooking the Pleistos gorge and the gulf of Itea beyond, and tasted the enormous juicy Amfissa olives, which were reputed to be among the best in the world.

But it was later, in their bedroom, on the square, iron-posted bed, with its rough cotton sheets and hand-woven spread, that Dion had made love to her, and beneath the spell of that enchanted place, Martha had had no mind to think of anything but him. The chances of her becoming pregnant had seemed so remote, and besides, intoxicated by his presence and drugged by the urgency of his kisses, she could have denied him nothing. She was on fire with love for him, satiated by his passion, and totally incapable of thinking beyond those ecstatic hours.

Of course, the enchantment had not lasted. Back in Athens his father had been fretting over an abortive attempt to gain control of a fleet of oil tankers, and Dion was despatched to the Persian Gulf to speak with some obscure ruler who had offered to make a deal with them. Martha's plea to go with her husband had been refused outright. A desert sheikdom was not the place for a woman, she was told, and she had returned to their apartment alone—and lonely.

The whisper of the wheels of Sarah's chair brought her abruptly back to the present, as her sister came out of the villa and propelled herself across the mosaic tiling towards her. Even Sarah had been unable to entirely avoid the mellowing warmth of the sun, and her skin was already acquiring a pinkish tinge. Sarah never tanned. She was too fair for that, but a healthy glow was warming her pale cheeks.

'Did you enjoy your rest?' Martha was self-conscious about the briefness of her shorts when compared to the cotton slacks that covered her sister's thin, useless legs. Swinging her feet to the floor, she sat up, and Sarah positioned the wheelchair close beside her.

'It's very hot,' declared Sarah peevishly, loosening another button of her white cotton shirt. 'I'll never get used to this climate. Never in a million years!'

'Of course you will.' Martha sighed. 'Why don't you do as Roger suggested, and go in the pool? At least the water——'

'If you think I'm going to make a laughing stock of myself by putting on a bathing suit, you're very much mistaken,' replied her sister shortly. 'You know Roger. He'd never let me forget it.'

'Oh, you're mistaken—honestly.' Martha leaned across and squeezed Sarah's arm. 'Roger is very fond of you, you know that. He only teases you, because you always rise to the bait. He doesn't mean any harm by it.'

Sarah sniffed. 'Roger wouldn't be half so friendly if you weren't Dionysus Myconos' wife,' she retorted, and Martha felt a surge of impatience.

'That's not true, and you know it!' she exclaimed. 'Good Lord! Do you really think he's been waiting for the last five years for Dion to come back into my life?'

Sarah shrugged. 'Well ...' She pulled a long face. 'You can't deny that without his encouragement we wouldn't be here now.'

Martha paused. 'No. No, that's true,' she agreed slowly. 'But let's face it, if anyone's responsible for Roger being here, it's you.'

Sarah nodded. 'I know. But even so——'

'Sarah, can't you just try and get something out of this?' Martha's tone was strained now. 'What you say about Roger encouraging me to speak to Dion's father is true, but you know, it's possible that sooner or later I'd have to tell Dion the truth.'

'Why?'

'Why?' Martha stared at the other girl. 'Why, because he's her father, of course. I have to think about Josy, too. She's my daughter, but her father's blood runs in her veins as well. How do you think she might have reacted in—say ten years' time, if she somehow learned who she was from someone else?'

Sarah hesitated. 'I think you underestimate yourself, Martha,' she said at last. 'And probably you underestimate Josy, too. Why, in her position I'd feel pretty strongly towards a man who abandoned my mother when I was born.'

'But Dion didn't do that, did he?' asked Martha impatiently. '*I* left him.'

'Because he disowned the child!'

'Oh, Sarah! It wasn't that simple. He—I—he was suspicious. He knew I'd been seeing Roger while I was in London. He never bothered to discover that you were the one Roger always wanted to see.'

'That's not true!' Sarah's cheeks flushed.

'It is true.' Martha pushed back the few tendrils of hair which had come loose on her forehead with a weary hand. 'We both know it. Somehow Dion got it into his head that Roger was the reason I was visiting London so often, and when the baby had red hair ...' She sighed. 'He didn't bother to consider that your hair is auburn, too, and that babies often lose all the hair they're born with.'

'But you told him!' exclaimed Sarah, still red-faced, and Martha gave her a sideways glance.

'You know what happened, Sarah. You know how stubborn I can be.' She sighed again. 'Maybe, after I'd had time to consider—if he'd come after me ... But he didn't. He told me his family stopped him, that they persuaded him to use the business as a palliative.' She bent her head. 'Some palliative!'

'I still think it was for the best,' said Sarah tautly. 'I don't know why you ever married him——'

'I *loved* him!' exclaimed Martha forcefully, lifting her head, and as she did so, she realised that Alex and Josy were walking barefoot across the patio towards them.

If Alex had heard what she said, he gave no sign of it, and Josy as usual was too absorbed in what she had to say to pay any attention to her mother's outburst.

'Mummy, Mummy!' she cried, as soon as Martha noticed her. 'I can swim, I can swim! Uncle Alex has taught me how to swim!'

Martha made a supreme effort and got to her feet. 'Why,

that's wonderful, darling,' she exclaimed, and really meant it, her eyes turning automatically to Alex for his reactions. 'Is it true? Can she really swim? It hardly seems possible, after only these few days.'

'She has a natural ability,' he answered modestly. 'And in these waters . . .' he smiled, 'anything is possible.'

'I swam right across the pool,' went on Josy importantly, and her uncle pulled a wry face.

'Let us say you kept afloat,' he teased, pulling a strand of wet dark hair that straggled over one of Josy's slim shoulders, and she turned to wrinkle her nose at him.

'Well, I think that's wonderful!' said Martha, relaxing as the tension between herself and Sarah eased. 'Now we won't have to worry about you falling in the pool accidentally. You won't drown, whatever happens.'

Josy basked in her mother's affection, and Alex turned his attention to Sarah. 'Good afternoon,' he greeted her politely. 'It is another lovely day, is it not? Are you sure you will not change your mind and join us in the water?'

Sarah shook her head, her lips tightening ominously. But she could not be rude to Alex, who had shown her nothing but kindness, and with a thin smile she said: 'I'd really rather not, if you don't mind. I'm quite happy sitting here.'

That was blatantly not true, but Alex did not argue, excusing himself instead on the pretext of having some telephone calls to make. Josy watched him go with faint regret, but then she turned to her mother, eager to induce her to come and watch her prowess.

'Will you come?' Martha asked her sister, but Sarah refused again, reaching for the magazine she had tucked down the side of her chair, and with a regretful shrug Martha followed her daughter through the garden to the swimming pool.

After watching Josy paddle her way across the pool a couple of times, Martha decided the little girl was tiring, and suggested instead that they drove down to the village.

Alex had put a station wagon at her disposal, and once or twice in the past days she and Josy and Sarah had taken drives about the island. The roads were not good—little more than cart tracks in places—but the outings were very enjoyable, enabling them to appreciate more fully the peace and isolation of Mycos.

Josy was quite willing to abandon the pool in favour of a trip to the village, and while the little girl changed her bathing suit for a pair of shorts and a matching vest, like her mother, Martha asked Sarah to join them.

'It's too hot,' Sarah repeated, looking up from her magazine rather impatiently. 'You go and get hot and sweaty. I'd rather sit here, in the shade, and enjoy what little breeze there is.'

'But, Sarah, you're not making any attempt to adapt——'

'I have no intention of adapting, as you call it. I didn't want to come here, and I don't intend to stay. Whatever you decide to do.'

Martha was in a rather distracted frame of mind as she and Josy drove down the narrow road to the village. She had hoped that once Sarah got here, once she began to enjoy the unaccustomed warmth and relaxation of the islands, she would try and make the best of the situation, but as always, her sister was taking a negative attitude towards everything, and even Dion's absence had made very little difference.

Happily, Josy was unaware of her feelings, and excitedly pointed out a donkey wearing a flower-covered hat, with its ears sticking through the straw, and the huge mounds of fruit and vegetables which were just being unloaded from a newly-arrived cargo boat.

'Can we stay and watch, Mummy?' she demanded, bouncing up and down in her seat, and good-humouredly Martha pulled on to the quayside, enjoying the placid, unhurried movements of the seamen. Here, away from the

villa, she could imagine they were in any Mediterranean
port, albeit a small one, without any of the problems the
Myconos family presented.

'Can't we get out, Mummy?' Josy persisted, not content
with just hanging out the window. 'I can't see!'

'I doubt if you'll see any more if we get out,' declared
Martha wryly, but she agreed that they could, and Josy
danced off along the wharf.

The sun was so hot, it was dazzling, and even Martha's
dark glasses did not entirely prevent the glare of sun on
blue, blue water. Standing there, shading her eyes with one
hand, she was completely unaware of the striking attraction
of her blonde beauty, but the man who had just dis-
embarked from the M.S. *Athena* was entirely aware of it.
Aware, too, of the envious glances cast in his direction, as
he excused himself from the crewmen he had been talking
to, and strode determinedly towards her, his jacket looped
round one finger and tossed casually over his shoulder.

Martha saw the man walking towards her, but she didn't
immediately pay him any attention, although it was unusual to find someone wearing formal clothes down at the
harbour. She did not associate him with her husband. When
Dion arrived, they would know about it, she was sure.
There would be the hum of the helicopter for a start, and
Alex rushing down to the airfield to pick him up. She
guessed it might possibly be one of the security guards,
though they usually kept a low profile, and she continued to
observe Josy, avidly watching the mechanical skills of the
driver of a small crane.

Only when the man reached her did she realise who it
was, and her lips parted in a disbelieving gasp. '*Dion!*' she
exclaimed, pulling off her sunglasses, as if their smoky
lenses might lie, and he inclined his head in a mocking
salute.

'The same,' he agreed, his narrowed eyes requiring no
protection, and in full view of the men on the quay, his

hands descended on her slim shoulders, and pulled her towards him.

'Dion—no,' she managed, before his mouth settled over hers and drove all resistance from her mind. It was too quick, too sudden, too unexpected for her to summon any defence, and her lips parted automatically beneath the expert pressure of his.

'Relax,' he said, against her mouth, his wine-scented breath almost suffocating her. 'Our friends think you are a welcoming committee. We would not like to disappoint them, would we?'

When she eventually fought free of him, she was flushed and breathless, the marks of his fingers clearly visible on her bare arms. She gazed up at him indignantly, searching for some reason for such an unprovoked attack, but all she found was speculation and mockery, and a certain cool-eyed triumph.

'Is this what you expect of me?' she demanded, in a low voice, trembling hands seeking the reassuring neatness of the knot she had secured on top of her head for coolness. 'Because if it is——'

'Where is Josy?' Dion interrupted her mildly, looking about him with all the assurance of the dominant male, and smilingly acknowledging the admiring glances of the fishermen. They could have no idea of the unequal battle they had just witnessed, Martha thought bitterly, wondering how Dion could behave so emotionally one minute and appear so emotionless the next. The truth was, it wasn't emotion at all, she decided frustratedly. He had been demonstrating his ownership, and she had been subdued.

Josy herself saw her father at that moment, and with a squeal of delight came skipping back along the quay towards them. She seemed to find being swept up into Dion's arms well to her liking, and with a feeling of helpless fury Martha climbed back into the station wagon. She deliberately chose the seat behind the steering wheel, hoping Dion

would question her position, but he didn't. Instead he carried Josy round the car, and climbed in beside her, with
Josy on his knee.

'Why didn't you let us know you were coming?' Josy demanded, voicing the question that trembled on her
mother's tongue, and Dion smiled.

'I wanted to surprise you—and I did,' he declared, with
a sidelong glance at his wife. 'Besides, the—er—helicopter
was needed for other things, and I enjoyed riding on
Andropolous's boat.'

'Andro—Andro—what?'

Josy was perplexed, and Dion pressed a teasing finger
on her nose as Martha vigorously started the car and swung
it round, away from the harbour. As she accelerated up the
hill away from the village, Dion endeavoured to explain the
pronunciation of the captain's name, and she felt an increasing surge of frustration at his easy companionship with the
child.

'I learned to swim today,' Josy told him proudly, as
Martha concentrated on negotiating the curves in the road.
'Uncle Alex taught me. Will you swim with me, Uncle
Dion? When we get home?'

'Home?' Dion echoed her word reflectively, and
Martha's lips compressed. How was she ever going to accept the ambiguousness of her position, even for Josy's
sake? she asked herself despairingly. She could not—she
would not—become Dion's plaything. If he thought he
could make love to her at will, treat her, as he had done
down at the harbour, he was very much mistaken. She had
come back to him for Josy's sake, and Josy's sake alone.
Somehow, tonight perhaps, she had to make her position
clear. It was a daunting thought, particularly remembering
the way her body reacted to the touch of his, but she would
do it—she *must* do it. For her own peace of mind ...

Alex was delighted to see his brother, and for once
Martha was glad of Sarah's incapacity. It gave them both a

chance to escape, but after seeing Sarah to her room, Martha made her way to the apartments she had been using. She did not need Sarah's pointed observations to realise that the situation at the villa was bound to change now, and she needed some time to compose herself before speaking to Dion again. Josy had been quite content to stay with her father, and Martha flung herself on the smoky damask silk that covered the bed and gazed unhappily up at the ceiling.

She had only been lying there about fifteen minutes however before the door opened, and she jerked up on her elbows, staring round in surprise. No one ever entered the room without knocking, except perhaps Josy, but it was not the little girl whose entry caused a fluttering of the curtains at the long windows. Her husband stood in the aperture, surveying the tense apprehension in her face, and then closed the doors behind him with a distinct, unnerving click.

Until that moment Martha had not considered whose apartments these might be. They were not the rooms she and Dion had used in the past, and she had assumed they were simply guest rooms. The adjoining dressing room could have belonged to either this room or the room next next door, and as all Dion's brothers spent time on the island, the contents of the wardrobes could have belonged to any one of them.

Only now was she convinced that these were Dion's apartments, that that was Dion's dressing room, and the muted blues and greys of their decoration were his choice and no one else's.

Still, she had to feign ignorance. 'What are you doing here?' she exclaimed, her eyes wide with protest. 'I'm trying to rest, if you don't mind, and I'd like to be left alone.'

For an answer, Dion raised his dark eyebrows and walked across the room, flinging his jacket on to a low basketwork chair, and unfastening the buttons of his waistcoat. Then he strolled to the windows, staring out silently at the view, and stretching Martha's nerves like violin strings, before turning back to face her.

'Alex tells me you have settled down quite well,' he remarked at last, shedding his waistcoat and starting on the buttons of his shirt. 'I am glad. You—and Josy—look much better. Very soon, there might even be a little more flesh on your bones.'

Martha swung her bare feet to the floor. 'What are you doing, Dion?' she demanded tremulously. 'This is my room. Will you please leave me alone!'

'Correction—this is *our* room,' retorted Dion calmly. 'It would not do for the servants to imagine our—how shall I say?—reunion is anything less than complete.'

Martha summoned all her energies to say tensely: 'You can't honestly expect me to—to sleep with you!'

'Why not?' Dion was removing his shirt now, and her senses stirred at the sight of his lean brown body. It would be so easy to give in to him, she thought desperately. *Too* easy. But if he wanted her, he would have to take her. She was giving nothing.

'Why not?' she echoed now, getting to her feet, unable to remain on the bed in the face of his statement. 'Why—why, because it's ludicrous, that's why not. You and I—we haven't seen one another for five years, Dion. We—we parted on—on unfriendly terms. You can't expect me to forget that!'

'Neither of us can forget the past,' he agreed heavily. 'And now, if you will excuse me. I need a shower, and a change of clothes. Then we will have more time for talk, no?'

Martha watched him go into the bathroom with a sense of disbelief. He really did intend that they should take up where they left off. She could hardly believe it. It could not be true. And whatever his intentions, she would not be *used* like this.

When the sound of the shower water reached her ears, she broke into jerky action. Pulling out her suitcases from their place inside the cupboard, she opened the wardrobe and began tumbling her clothes into them. Skirts and dresses, blouses and sweaters, all were stuffed inside with the least amount of effort, and if they got creased, then she would have to iron them later, she decided, without really caring. She would share Josy's room. She wouldn't mind. And if she did—well, perhaps later on, another room might be found for her.

She was so intent on what she was doing that she was unaware that the water had stopped running, and she swung round guiltily when Dion's angry voice addressed her.

'What do you think you are doing?' he demanded, striding towards her menacingly, dark and disturbing in a black-figured robe that fell to his ankles. 'Do you think I would allow you to remain in another room, always supposing you had succeeded in leaving this one?'

Martha straightened, a handful of underwear clasped foolishly in her hands, but his fingers around her wrist made her drop the fragile shield. 'You can't force me to sleep in here,' she insisted, tilting her head. 'I can share with Josy, until—until——'

'Yes?' he interrupted coldly. 'Until what? Until I return to Athens, or until you decide you *want* to share my bed again?'

'That's not likely to happen, is it?' she retorted, trying not to be intimidated by the fury in his face, and his eyes narrowed speculatively.

'No?' he enquired, with deceptive mildness, and her knees shook alarmingly.

'No,' she repeated, steeling herself to face his anger, and was disarmed once again by his sudden change of mood. With an ease born of long practice he released her wrist, his hands seeking her waist and drawing her insistently towards him. Beneath the thin robe his body was firm and muscular, but she had hardly time to register this before his hands slid intimately to the cuffs of her shorts, curving over the smooth flesh at the tops of her legs. She was moulded to the contours of his body, made aware of every stirring muscle, and then robbed of all breath by the stifling pressure of his mouth.

'Dion ...' Her choking plea went unheard beneath the demanding urgency of his kiss, and as before, weakness enveloped her. It had been so long since any man had kissed her, and no man but Dion had ever kissed her with such passion. She wanted to protest, to hold out against him, but her awakening senses blinded her reason, and with a feeling of abandonment her arms wound themselves around his neck.

Then, just when she thought he was going to lift her up and carry her to the bed, he drew back, taking her arms from around his neck and pressing them gently but firmly to her sides.

'Now,' he said, and there was an edge of sarcasm to his voice, 'unpack those things like a good girl, and I will go and dress for dinner.'

Martha clenched her fists, but she didn't say anything, and with a faint cold smile he walked towards the door of his dressing room. He had done it again, she thought incredulously, and there seemed to be little she could do about it.

'Oh—and by the way,' he paused in the open doorway, '*we* will be returning to Athens in three days.'

'We?' Martha couldn't prevent the shocked ejaculation, and he nodded.

'You—and I,' he agreed smoothly. 'There is a party which I wish you to attend with me, and of course, my mother wishes to see you once again.'

Martha's head started to move from side to side. 'I—I can't leave Josy——'

'Josy has been—how do you say—taken care of, no? I

have employed an English nanny for her, which I thought would please you, and it is time she learned that you will not constantly be at her beck and call.'

Martha was bewildered. 'Dion——'

'Later,' he averred firmly, and the dressing room door closed behind him.

Left to herself, Martha unpacked her clothes again almost without being aware of it. She had too many other things to think about, not least this proposed trip to Athens. Why did Dion want her to accompany him to this party, wherever it was, and why should his mother want to see her again? Surely, he had explained why he was taking her back. He couldn't really expect them to behave as if nothing had happened. It was not possible. And her nerves tightened at the prospect of meeting Dion's parents after the way Aristotle had spoken to her, here, at the villa.

Then there were her clothes to think about. Her wardrobe had once been quite extensive, but time and changing fashions had narrowed it down to a couple of cotton dresses, one or two suits, and a selection of skirts and tops. Nothing suitable for a party in Athens, not the kind of party that the Myconos's attended anyway.

The other arrangements Dion had made she viewed with even less enthusiasm. An English nanny! What did he mean? Who was this person he had employed, and when was she expected to arrive? And what would Sarah think when she discovered that Martha was expected to walk out on her?

Sitting down on the edge of the bed, she buried her face in her hands and was still sitting that way when Dion came back into the room. She didn't want to look up at him, but her attitude of dejection smacked too strongly of an appeal for his pity, and that was the last thing she wanted to convey. In a dark green velvet dinner packet and black pants, he looked every inch the successful tycoon she knew him to be, and a sense of inadequacy and overwhelming defeat gripped her. How could she fight him, when he held Josy's happiness in his hands?

'Do I take it you intend to eat dinner in that outfit?' he asked mockingly, and she got automatically to her feet.

'I have to supervise Josy's bath,' she said defensively, twisting her hands together, and he acknowledged this with a frowning inclination of his head.

'Only until tomorrow,' he amended. 'The good Miss Powell arrives tomorrow, and from then on she will attend to Josy's personal requirements.'

Martha's jaw stiffened. 'But I like looking after her myself,' she objected.

Dion shrugged. 'As I have said, you will be accompanying me to Athens. Do not argue, Martha. I have made up my mind.'

'And I have no opinions?'

'You will be consulted, of course——'

'When?'

'When I consider it necessary,' he stated quietly. 'And now I suggest you—do what you have to. I have business to discuss with Alex. We will meet again at dinner.'

The door closed behind him leaving Martha feeling even more distraught than before. What was she going to do? How was she going to fight him? Was she condemned to submission until Josy was old enough to choose for herself?

CHAPTER SEVEN

THE sunlight filtering through the slatted blinds awakened Martha. It was still very early, but she no longer had any desire for sleep. She was too restless, too confused to lie there, at the mercy of her anxieties, and drawing in a trembling breath she flung back the silken sheet which was all that had covered her.

The room was limpid amber in the morning light, the hazy blue curtains at the windows melting into the shadows. The mahogany chest and matching dressing table looked almost golden as they reflected the sun's rays, the polished blocks of the floor shafting dust motes in a transparent cascade.

As she padded across to the windows, she glanced back half apprehensively at the bed, but she was alone. She had been alone all night, and the trembling anticipation which had kept her awake until the early hours had heralded nothing more than a restless night's sleep.

Jerking on the cord, she half opened the blinds, gazing out broodingly at the colour-washed garden. She felt a little sick and headachy, a sense of bewilderment and disbelief vying with the relief she knew she ought to be feeling. Why hadn't Dion come to bed? Where had he slept? Had he slept at all? And if so, what had all that conversation been about earlier?

It would be foolish to feel disappointed, but she was confused, and her tired brain refused to find reasons for his absence. He had intended to come, she was sure of it—though could she honestly be sure of anything in this uncertain situation?

Reviewing the events of the previous evening, she had had no reason to doubt his intentions. But then she had not spent a lot of time with him—with any of them—involved as she had been with Josy's little upset.

No doubt the heat, and too much exercise, had been responsible for her sickness and irritability, and Martha had spent most of the evening attending to her daughter's needs. Dion had suggested that one of the servants could attend to her, but Martha would not hear of it, and as always when she opposed Dion, Sarah came to her aid.

'A child needs her mother at a time like this,' she declared, when Martha was called away from the table for the second time. Josy had had her meal earlier, as had become her habit, but for some reason she was hot and restless, and a gastric upset had left her pale and tearful. 'You can't expect Martha to leave Josy in the hands of strangers, Dion. She's cared for her for too long. They're too close.'

'Oh, I agree.' Dion's meaning was chillingly clear. 'They are too close, much too close, but I intend to change that in the not-too-distant future.'

Martha, hurrying away from the table, had heard his remarks with a sense of alarm. Was that why her husband was so keen that she should accompany him to Athens? Was his intention to wean them apart so gradually that neither of them would necessarily be aware of the separation? Was this English nanny intended to substitute for herself ultimately? Was his whole plan of taking her back only a temporary arrangement so that Josy should not be too upset when the real break came?

With thoughts like these for company, Martha was in no state to act objectively, and Josy had responded to her over-indulgence with childish abandon, taking advantage of her mother's anxiety, and making more of her upset than was really necessary.

When Andros came to tell her that Josy was calling for her a fourth time, however, even Roger got the message.

'She's playing you up, Martha, can't you see?' he exclaimed, breaking off a conversation he had been having with Alex about the excavation at Akrotiri to catch her arm as she went by. 'You know what children are like. She knows her—well, she knows that your husband is here. She wants attention, that's all. Stop giving in to her.'

'You are right.' It was Dion who spoke, getting up from his seat and coming round the table towards them. 'I will go and have a few words with her. Sit down again, Martha. Leave this to me.'

'No——'

Martha began to protest, but Roger would not let go of her arm and she stood impotently by as Dion disappeared into the house. 'Relax,' Roger advised her firmly, his eyes sending her a message of warning. 'Let Dion speak to her. That's what she needs, isn't it? A—*man*'s hand.'

'Don't you mean a father's?' demanded Sarah angrily. 'Martha, can't you see what Dion's doing? He's trying to usurp your place with Josy——'

'That is nonsense!' It was Alex who spoke now, his youthful features hard with resentment. 'Why should not my brother speak with his own daughter? For she is his daughter, even I can see that!'

'Then it's a pity you didn't see it sooner,' retorted Sarah, equally resentfully. 'Martha's looked after Josy alone for years without any help from the Myconos family. Why should you assume she needs any help now?'

'Sarah, please ...'

Martha's weary protest was hardly noticed as Alex rose to his feet. 'Your sister left my brother, Miss Connell,' he snapped harshly, 'not the other way about. It almost killed him, do you know that? Do you also know that he has gone against every recommendation of his family in bringing *you* here!'

Martha at last pulled away from Roger and resumed her seat. But the atmosphere around the table was no longer sympathetic to casual conversation, and she was glad when the meal was over and she could escape. Dion had returned to his seat with the news that Josy seemed much recovered, and when Martha peeped into her room on her way to her own, she did not stir. Obviously, whatever Dion had said, she had responded to it, and her spirits sank a little lower as she sought the no-longer-inviolable sanctuary of her bedroom.

But a sanctuary it had remained, throughout the long hours of the night, even though her thoughts were not the calm and tranquil ones associated with such a retreat. Adding Alex's denunciation to her husband's humiliating attitude brought a feeling of almost overwhelming despair, and she realised she had been mistaken in thinking Dion's brother had forgiven her. He was being polite, that was all, for Josy's sake, the innocent pawn in this game of chance.

And now it was morning, the morning of the day the English nanny would arrive, and Martha felt totally incapable of handling it. What would this woman be like? Young or old? Friendly or aggressive? Experienced or inexperienced, as she was herself?

With a summoning of determination, she resolved to think positively. Surely if Dion had only intended her to stay for a short time, he would not have been so adamant that she should give up her job at the university. Unless he had wanted to hurt her in that way, too, knowing that such good jobs were hard to find ...

She had no way of proving her suspicions, and deciding she could grow old with worry, she tossed off her cotton nightdress, and went into the bathroom to wash and clean her teeth. Then, realising that what she really needed was something to clear her head, she put on the navy bikini she had bought to go to the Scillies the previous year, and wrapping one of the huge bath towels about her, left her room.

The pool was already occupied, however, and she was half tempted to draw back before whoever it was had seen her. But giving in to those kind of fears was not part of her new determination, and although her knees were trembling, she trod through the trellised archway that gave access to the pool area.

It was not her husband, she saw at once, but Alex who was pacing his length across its translucent surface, and when he saw her he immediately turned on to his back and kicked lazily towards the side.

'*Esti, kalimera*, Martha,' he called, a lazy smile curving his mouth. 'Am I to have company?'

Martha hesitated only a moment, and then shed the fluffy towel, allowing it to fall to the mosaic tiles that surrounded the pool. 'Do you want company?' she asked, stepping to the rim, and he swam easily towards her, splashing water up on to her legs.

'Your company?' he asked. 'But of course.'

Martha still lingered. 'Even—even after what you said last night?' she ventured.

'Last night?' He frowned, levering himself up on to the tiles beside her, his dripping body scented with salt from the water that was pumped up from the ocean. 'What did I say last night?'

Martha bent her head, tentatively dipping a toe into the cold depths. 'You know,' she insisted. 'About—about me being here.'

'You?' Alex shook his head. 'I do not understand. I am glad you are here. This is where you belong, where you have always belonged.'

Martha shook her head. 'But when you were speaking to Sarah——'

'Ach, Sarah!' Alex's jaw hardened instantly, and she saw again the expression he had worn the night before. 'Do not speak of yourself in the same breath with your sister. She has done everything in her power to destroy your marriage.

She is the one who should not be here. *She* is the person my family most abhors.'

'Oh!' Martha could not deny the shiver of unease that still swept over her at the words. Obviously, the Myconos's had made Sarah their scapegoat. They could not believe that anyone could prefer freedom to life with a man who distrusted her so much, he even denied his own daughter's existence. They had needed someone to blame, and they had blamed Sarah. But it was all wrong. They should have blamed *her*!

'Alex, honestly——' she began now, but he silenced her with his finger across her lips.

'No more,' he said. 'Let us not spoil the day by thinking of the past. Dion has said we must forget it, and I want to do so.'

Martha drew an uneven breath. Alex could be so serious at times, and right now he was looking at her with an intensity that reminded her only too well of Dion at his most appealing.

'All right,' she murmured, unwilling to prolong the emotiveness of his expression, and his eyes softened into gentleness.

'You look so anxious,' he said, touching her cheek with damp fingers. 'Do not be so. Everything will turn out for the best, you will see.'

Martha wished she could believe him, but at least in the next fifteen minutes or so, she forgot her troubles in the pure enjoyment of the water. It was so soft, so buoyant, one hardly needed to use one's legs at all. Sarah should try it, she thought, not voicing the thought for fear of provoking any further outbursts from Alex, but she would try harder to get her sister interested, if only because of the therapy it would be for her.

They had pulled themselves out of the water and were lying by the side of the pool, discussing Alex's abandoned hopes of becoming a lecturer, when Dion appeared. To his eyes, their closeness must have appeared suspect, Martha thought, herself lying flat on her back, letting the sun dry the moisture from her body, and Alex on his stomach beside her, chin propped on one hand as he explained his reasons for obeying his father. But her husband showed no particular signs of annoyance, coming to stand over them, lean and masculine in cream denim pants and a tight-fitting cotton shirt.

'*Ya*, Dion!' Alex greeted him familiarly, making no attempt to rise. 'We thought you were going to sleep all day, did we not, Martha?' He grinned. 'See, your wife has already swum the Hellespont twice over.'

'Alex . . .'

Martha cast an impatient look in his direction as she sat up, but Dion's expression gave her no clue to what he was thinking. 'I can see she looks a little tired,' he remarked, squatting down beside them. 'But after Miss Powell's arrival she will find life much easier.'

Martha refused to meet the challenge in those dark brown irises, but she heard Alex ask what time the nursemaid was due to arrive and waited tensely for Dion's reply.

'About noon, I would imagine,' he said at last. 'You have met her, of course. Perhaps you could reassure Martha that she is not the gorgon she apparently thinks her.'

Martha's eyes turned to Alex, as he levered himself back on to his heels. 'That is true,' he nodded. 'I have met the lady. She is most charming, I am sure you will like her.'

Martha was equally sure she would not, but she could hardly say so, and ignoring Dion's outstretched hand, she got to her feet unaided, and went to wrap herself in the enveloping folds of the towel.

Dion straightened and Alex got to his feet, too, and she felt their eyes upon her as she quickly tucked the towel, sarong-style, about her. She wondered if Alex imagined they had spent the night together, and their present attitude was the result of some misunderstanding they had

had. Whatever, she needed the uncomplicated company of Josy or Roger, or even Sarah, to restore her sense of balance, and with a faint smile of dismissal, she left them.

Dion came into the bedroom as she was brushing her hair, preparatory to plaiting it into its single braid. It was disconcerting that he could just walk in on her uninvited and unannounced, but she succeeded in biting back her resentment, continuing with her task as if he wasn't there. She wasn't going to give him the opportunity to taunt her over the reasons why he had stayed away the night before, though her fingers still trembled as she fumbled to divide the silky strands.

'Leave it,' he commanded, after watching her struggles for several disturbing minutes. 'I prefer that you leave it loose. Do this for me.'

If anything could have been designed to make Martha want to braid her hair all the more, his words would have fitted the description. Ignoring him, she made another attempt to separate the silky curtain into three equal sections, and then stiffened into immobility when he came up behind her.

'I said leave it,' he repeated quietly, reaching past her to lift the brush, and pushing her hands aside, restored it to its honey-gold smoothness. 'If you must control it for coolness, use a piece of elastic, or a ribbon. Much as I admire your youthful appearance, I do not like your hair so severely confined.'

Martha swallowed convulsively. 'Your opinion is of no interest to me,' she declared.

'No?' he shrugged. 'But I like to thread my fingers through it—like this,' he tossed the brush aside to comb long fingers through the silky strands, 'and to bury my face in its softness——'

He bent his head to the nape of her neck, and panic that once again he was playing with her flared along Martha's nerves. With a little cry she jerked herself away from him, and saw the mirror image of his amusement reflected in the glass.

'What is wrong?' he asked, surveying her in mocking appraisal. 'You do not mind me touching you, do you? Or are you perhaps disappointed that I did not take advantage of my—what do you call it?—marital rights last night, no?'

Martha's fingers hurt almost more than his cheek must have done, she thought, rubbing them painfully after the slap she had so impulsively delivered. What would he do now? she wondered, her eyes darting uneasily about the room, and then returning to his unfortunate cheek in reluctant penitence.

'So,' he said at last, lifting one hand to touch the white markings of her fingers that stood out in cold relief against the hotness of his skin. 'Does that make you feel better? Does that—assuage the bitterness you feel when I prove to you that you are not immune to me, whatever you might wish?'

Martha's breathing felt constricted, and it was with some difficulty that she got out her next words. 'You—you think you're so clever, don't you?' she cried. 'Just because you can —arouse me. Well, I'm an emancipated woman, not a child. Like you, I have—needs, and appetites. That does not mean *only* you can satisfy them!'

She did not know how she had found the nerve to make such a statement, and she waited apprehensively for his response. But he chose not to argue. With derision curving his mouth he turned away, and walking indolently towards the door, let himself out without another word.

His departure left her feeling drained and exhausted. After the night she had just spent, she needed affection and sympathy, not these continual battles of the senses, and although she might deny her attraction towards him, it was a foolish affectation when he could exert such tremendous power over her.

It had always been like that, right from the very beginning, she reflected defeatedly, wondering at the perversity of fate. The holiday she and Sarah had spent in Rhodes had been deliberately devoid of attachments, but that last evening, when she had allowed Sarah to persuade her to accept the invitation of two waiters from their hotel, how could she have known what was about to happen? There was a disco, they said, at one of the small villages between Rhodes and Kremasti, and the two girls had decided it might be fun. But it hadn't been fun at all. Just rather sordid and embarrassing, the two young Greeks imagining that the English girls would be game for anything. Of course, as soon as they discovered they were not, they took off, leaving Martha and Sarah to find their own way back to the hotel, which wasn't easy, when there were no taxis to be had, and neither of them spoke sufficient Greek at that time to make themselves understood.

They had eventually decided to walk, but then Sarah had twisted her ankle and Martha had become convinced they were going in the wrong direction, and that sense of panic that everyone experiences when faced with a nightmare situation had begun to grip them.

The villa they eventually came upon lay in a wooded valley, some distance from the main coast road. It was the dogs which had alerted the villa's owner to trespassers in his grounds, and pure chance that Dion should have been dining there that evening. By then Sarah could hardly walk at all, and Martha had no hesitation about approaching the occupant and asking if they might ring for a taxi from there.

Remembering the way Dion had come to their rescue brought an unwilling weakness to her limbs. That he could speak English had been relief enough, without his insisting on driving them back to their hotel himself. He had picked Sarah up in his strong arms and carried her into the villa, and his anxious hosts had quickly found cold water and bandages to bind her ankle.

Frowning now, Martha reflected that that was when Sarah had convinced herself that Dion was attracted to her. She had given no thought to the fact that he was merely being polite, that he would have done the same for anyone in similar circumstances. She had been fascinated by the lean capability of his hands, the quiet efficiency that accomplished so much without apparent effort.

Martha herself had treated the whole affair with a certain amount of amusement once the worst was over. After all, it had been an adventure, something they could talk about once they got home to England, certainly nothing to be taken too seriously. She rode back to the hotel in the rear seat of Dion's sleek limousine, deliberately avoiding the obvious comparisons between this attractive stranger and the two boys they had started out with, keeping herself immune from his dark good looks and his identity.

When he arrived the following morning to enquire after Sarah's ankle, and to assure himself that they had both recovered from their ordeal, it had become harder to evade the searching intensity of his gaze. He spoke mostly to Sarah, but he looked at her, and Martha's palms moistened even now, remembering that slumbrous stare.

Of course, it had not ended there—even though, when they flew back to England that same afternoon, Martha had assured herself that they had seen the last of him. Within a week Dion was in London, possessed of their address, and making himself at home at Maxwell Grove, as if he had lived in such modest surroundings all his life.

Sarah was delighted at first, believing he was attracted to her, and making special efforts with her hair and clothes. Martha kept out of the way as much as she could. After learning of his identity, she was convinced he was merely amusing himself at their expense, and the fact that he might be serious never even crossed her mind.

Until the evening he arrived to find Sarah was out, at a committee meeting. She had been quite an enthusiastic member of the local historical society in those days, she and Roger had always had that in common, and besides, she had told Martha that Dion had had to fly back to Athens that afternoon, and had promised to ring on his return.

When Martha opened the door to him that evening they had both known why he was there. There was no possibility that she was mistaken. It was there in his face, in his expression, in the smouldering passion in his eyes, and before the door had closed behind him she was in his arms.

Such memories were painful, she discovered, as her teeth dug deeply into her lower lip. They had been so eager, so hungry for one another, so completely absorbed with the physical expression of their love. And Dion was so expert when it came to seducement, so adroit at the art of intimacy. With his mouth plundering the sweetness of hers, teaching her the meaning of possession, she had been helpless in his hands, fervent and willing to give whatever he wanted of her.

The fact that he had not taken her on that occasion had been his choice, not hers. Even though he had parted her shirt and exposed the throbbing peaks of her breasts to his caress, he had not made love to her, and she had felt the first aching in her thighs that only his penetration could assuage. She had touched his body, of course, ardently delighting in the unaccustomed freedom, and reluctantly he had removed her probing fingers, assuring her wryly that only by this abstinence could he be expected to keep his head.

Telling Sarah had not been easy. Her reaction had ranged from an immediate one of tight-smiling indifference, to complete and outright disapproval. She had never taken Dion seriously, she denied, when Martha tried to defend herself later. He had no intention of marrying an *English* girl, she insisted, he was only playing with her, and Martha ought to know that Greek millionaires did not seriously get involved with doctors' receptionists.

Of course, time proved her wrong, but Martha wondered now at the risks she had taken. Dion's self-restraint had not lasted long in the face of their urgent need for one another, and within a week she was going to bed with him, unable to resist his disturbing attraction. They had been unable to leave one another alone, and he had taken her to meet his family, with his own plans for their wedding already clear in his mind.

Naturally, she supposed, the Myconos's had been appalled. She was so different from the wife they must have wanted for their eldest son. She was subjected to the most stringent interrogation whenever Dion was out of the room, but in spite of everything they had been undeterred.

In fact, their marriage had eventually been sponsored by his family, and not hers. There were so many people the Myconos's wanted to invite, and although Martha had been terrified at the thought of such an occasion, with Dion beside her, it had not seemed so frightening. It had been a wonderful day, a glorious wedding, the guests thronging the marquee which had been set up in the grounds of Aristotle's villa in Athens; and afterwards, an equally splendid honeymoon, spent in the tropical seclusion of Bali.

Sighing now, she surveyed her reflection in the leaved mirrors of the dressing table. Would she have stayed away from Dion if it had not been for Sarah? she wondered unhappily. Would she have maintained her independence without her sister's support? Whatever, nothing could alter the fact that Dion had stayed away from her, that he had accepted her departure as final, and had only taken her back now to gain control of Josy and to satisfy some streak of cruelty that dominated him.

The door opened again, but this time her wide-eyed look

of apprehension was for nothing. It was her daughter who came into the room, tousle-haired and adorable in candy-striped pyjamas.

'I slept in,' she announced, knuckling her eyes as she looked around the room. Then she frowned as she added: 'And Sophia says I must get dressed because there's a lady coming today, to look after me and Auntie Sarah while you go away with Uncle Dion. You're not going away, are you, Mummy? You won't go away again without taking me?'

Martha's spirits sank. She had hoped to break that particular piece of news to Josy in her own way, but she should have anticipated the garrulity of the servants. Gossip was a way of life, and Sophia, one of the young maids from the village, would not consider her words in any way controversial.

'As a matter of fact, I might be going away—just for a day or two,' Martha finished hastily, as Josy's eyes filled with concern. 'With—with Uncle Dion, as Sophia says. But I shan't be away for long, and Auntie Sarah is staying here, of course.'

Josy's lips assumed a downward slant. 'Then there is a lady coming to look after us. Who is she? Will she be like Mrs Bennett?'

Martha wished now she had questioned Alex about the nursemaid, but she hadn't, and taking a chance, she said: 'Someone like that, I suppose, darling. I'm sure she'll be very nice. Uncle—Uncle Dion chose her, and you know he wouldn't choose someone you wouldn't like.'

Josy sniffed. 'What's her name?'

'That I don't know.' Martha put her hands on the little girl's slim shoulders in a gesture of reassurance. 'But we'll find out very soon, I promise.'

Josy still looked upset, and Martha cupped her pale cheeks, a hangover from the previous evening's sickness, with gentle hands. 'Honey, don't worry. I—I may not go away, after all. It's all—in the balance. Now, hurry along and wash your face and clean your teeth, and we'll have breakfast together.'

As at dinner, the members of the household usually gathered for breakfast round the glass-topped table on the patio. At this hour of the morning the air was warm and redolent with the perfume of the flowers that grew on the terraces below. The moistness of the early hours was giving way to the heat of the morning, and the faint haze on the horizon heralded another glorious day. The view from the patio was quite magnificent, and in spite of everything, Martha always found pleasure in sitting there, drinking her orange juice and allowing the humming of the cicadas to wash over her.

Andros had placed a centrepiece of long-stemmed red roses in the middle of the table, and when Martha came out of the villa Alex rose from the seat and offered her one with a lazy smile.

'For Aphrodite,' he teased, touching her chin with his tender petals, and Martha wondered whether he was deliberately trying to annoy his brother. Dion had risen at her appearance, too, but after a moment he resumed his seat, studying the financial pages of a newspaper as he bit into a crisply baked croissant.

Martha accepted Alex's gallantry with a certain amount of impatience, and then, as she seated herself, said: 'Sophia's told Josy that this—this nursemaid is coming. She's quite upset about it.'

Dion looked up at this, but his eyes were cool and guarded. '*Then pirazi. Min anissihite.* She had to know sooner or later.'

Martha's lips tightened. 'I would prefer to have told her myself.'

'Why?' He shrugged. 'I will explain the situation to her.'

'Not as you explained it to me, I hope,' Martha retorted, unable to hide the emotion in her voice, and Alex pulled a wry face as he resumed his seat.

Fortunately, perhaps, Roger appeared at that moment long and gangly in his khaki shirt and shorts. His skin was already weathered by hours spent in the open air, but he looked well and energetic, and Martha told herself she was glad for him. Even so, she could not forget that it was he who had encouraged her to write to Aristotle, and precipitated this bewildering state of affairs.

'Alex tells me you have not yet been successful in discovering any connection between Mycos and Thera,' Dion remarked, folding his newspaper, unperturbed by Martha's previous outburst. 'Is it a disappointment?'

'Hell, no,' Roger grinned, helping himself to coffee. 'You don't know what it means to me, having the place to myself. It's fascinating. The rock formations alone provide an intriguing study, and with Alex's directions I found a cove yesterday and did some underwater exploration. Perhaps you wouldn't mind if I sent for my scuba-diving gear. I'd like to go a little deeper than the scope of my lungs allows.'

Dion was sympathetic. 'There is no need for you to send to England for that kind of equipment,' he remarked. 'We have tanks and suits here, on the island. Alex and I, and my brother Nikos, have all enjoyed the sport at one time or another. I will get Niarchos to give you what you need.'

'I say!' Roger was overwhelmed. 'I don't know how to thank you.'

Dion's smile was friendly. 'Enjoy,' he advised, getting to his feet. 'And now, if you will all excuse me . . .'

After he had left them, Roger continued to marvel at his good fortune. 'That's some bloke!' he averred, spreading apricot conserve on his toast. 'I'll never be able to thank him.'

His eyes sought Martha's, seeking confirmation, but she concentrated on her own meal with rather less enthusiasm. It was typical of Dion to be so generous, but she refused to admit it. He had always been willing to share his possessions—except when she was concerned.

CHAPTER EIGHT

MARTHA heard the helicopter fly over the villa at about eleven-thirty, and her nerves tightened. So the English nanny was arriving ahead of schedule, and she supposed Dion would expect her to be around to welcome her. Even Josy's curiosity had been aroused during the course of the morning, taking the place of her previous apprehension, and Martha realised if she was completely honest with herself she would admit that her own antipathy towards the newcomer had hardened as her daughter's enthusiasm increased. For so long she had been the centre of the little girl's world, the focus for her affections, and if Dion succeeded in destroying these things, what would she have left?

In consequence, she had spent the morning in Sarah's company, preferring her unconcealed antagonism to everyone else's interest. Of course, her sister had her own reasons for condemning the nursemaid's arrival. Josy had artlessly explained what Sophia had told her, and Sarah had immediately withdrawn behind a barrier of cold disapproval. She didn't have to tell Martha what she thought of the situation. It was evident in every movement, every gesture, every contemptuous sigh she uttered.

However, the lowering helicopter drove her to make some comment, and catching Martha's eye, she said: 'Aren't you going down to meet her? I heard the car leave a few minutes ago. I'd have thought you'd be curious to see the woman who's apparently going to take your place.'

Martha shifted uncomfortably on the lounger. 'You're

exaggerating, Sarah,' she said. 'This is Dion's idea of making life easier for me. He doesn't understand that I prefer to take care of Josy myself.'

'Huh!' Sarah sounded incredulous. 'If you believe that, you'll believe anything. You know perfectly well what Dion's game is. He's trying to come between you two. He knows that so long as Josy relies on you, he'll never stand a chance of taking her from you. But if he can get her used——'

'Oh, stop it, Sarah!' With a helpless gesture, Martha got to her feet, fists clenching and unclenching as she tried not to believe what her sister was saying. 'It's not like that. I— Dion wants me to accompany him to Athens. He wanted to be sure Josy would be well looked after while I was away, that's all.'

Sarah's lips curled. 'Really? You mean to tell me she couldn't have stayed with Roger and me for a few days?' She shook her head. 'This is no temporary measure, Martha. This is for keeps. You don't employ an English nursemaid for a week's engagement.'

Martha expelled her breath uneasily. Sarah was only voicing what she herself suspected, and that was why she found it so hard to take. She didn't want to hear her anxieties put into words, to face the unpalatable facts that had to be considered. What was Dion's game? And how long could she take it?

'I'm going for a walk,' she said at last, brushing down the skirt of her cotton sundress. She had worn the dress deliberately, unwilling to appear before Dion in the scanty shorts she had been wearing on his arrival, though its full skirts hid much of her slender limbs from the warmth of the sun. It was at least two years old, and its colour had faded, but it gave her a measure of protection from his mocking eyes.

Sarah looked surprised now. 'Where are you walking to?' she exclaimed. 'It's almost lunchtime.'

Martha shrugged, avoiding her eyes. 'Just for a walk,' she replied, already crossing the patio. 'See you later.'

Beyond the cultivated grounds of the villa, the hillside was covered with stretches of gorse, starred here and there with clumps of wild flowers. The perfumes of jasmine and hibiscus mingled with the sharper scents of lime and lemon groves, and the pervading tang of pine drifted down from the wooded slopes. Martha, bending to pick a tiny crimson-petalled blossom, thought how beautiful it all was, and how poignant it might well seem in retrospect.

The walls of the monastery loomed above her, and ignoring the impulse to turn back and face whatever was to come, she stepped up to the crumbling walls, noticing with pleasure that the vines still grew wild along the cloisters. Bunches of grapes hung lusciously above her, the purple and white garland of bougainvillaea disguising much of the decaying stonework. Grass grew between the flags that had once pointed the way to the chapel of St Demetrius, and the well was moss-covered, the water no longer drinkable.

Yet despite its air of desolation and neglect, it was a peaceful place, a sanctuary, and Martha spent some time exploring its quiet walks and sheltered terraces, where once the monks had striven to make a living from the soil. Martha wished her life was as uncomplicated as theirs, automatically bending her head as the noisy whir of the helicopter's propellers swept almost aggressively over the monastery.

It was almost one o'clock as she made the descent to the villa again, but she refused to feel deterred. She had every right to go for a walk if she wished, and nothing Dion could say would stop her. If he had expected her to be there to greet his latest acquisition, it was just too bad, and this woman, whoever she was, need not imagine she was going to have it all her own way.

She heard voices on the patio as she circled the gardens, but they were too distant for her to distinguish any particular tone. Avoiding them she let herself in through the french doors of one of the reception rooms, and made her way to her bedroom without encountering anyone other than a housemaid.

She halted in the doorway, however, aghast at the sight that greeted her eyes. The room seemed full of people, although in effect there were only two servant girls there, but the floor of the room, and every available chest and chair was overflowing with cartons and boxes, spilling dresses and skirts, pants and blouses, shoes and lingerie, in every imaginable style and shade.

'What is going on?' she gasped, gazing about her in bewilderment, and then realising the girls did not understand her, added: *'Ti ine afto?'*

'Your new wardrobe, *kiria*,' one of the girls replied in her own language. 'Kirios Dionysus asked us to unpack for you.'

'Did he?' Martha stared helplessly at the magenta swathe of a heavy silk evening gown.

'Ne, kiria,' the other girl nodded, smiling slyly. 'So many beautiful things. Kirios Dionysus must love you very much, *ohi*?'

Martha bit hard on her lower lip. She doubted very much whether love had anything to do with it. Dion did not wish to feel ashamed of her, that was all, and obviously he had noticed the deficiencies of her present wardrobe.

But so many things, as the girl had said! When had they been purchased? How had he known what she needed? What size to buy?

The answer was simple. Dion knew women. And he had obviously guessed she was one size smaller now than she had been when she was his wife. And as far as deciding what she wanted was concerned, he had apparently bought everything—from stockings through to the fur cape one of the girls was presently holding against her cheek.

Martha felt stunned. It was like being deprived of her breath. She didn't know what to say, what to do—and in addition to this, she had still to meet Josy's nursemaid.

She sensed rather than heard the footsteps coming along the corridor, and she knew who it was even before he came up behind her, and slipped a proprietorial hand around her waist. His fingers pressed possessively on her stomach, and before she could offer any possible opposition, he dismissed the two housemaids with a peremptory word of command. They slipped past, smiling knowingly, but after they had gone chattering down the passage, Martha turned on Dion with an angry protest.

'What is all this?' she demanded, walking into the middle of the floor, spreading her hands in expressive distaste. 'Are my clothes not good enough for you? Are you ashamed of me, is that it? Have I to be hung like a Christmas tree with the fruits of your exploitation?' She forgot completely her own anxieties about going to Athens, her earlier doubts about what she might wear. All she could see now was another demonstration of his control over her, another string for her to dance to his tune.

Dion did not immediately say anything. He closed the door and leaned back against it, allowing her to spend herself in useless fury, and then he said quietly: 'Where have you been?'

'Where have I been?' Martha moved her shoulders in careless indifference. 'Does it matter? Or do I have to account to you for every minute of my time as well? Would you like to know when I eat, when I change, when I go to the bathroom——'

'Be silent!' For once, she realised she had caught him on the raw, and she refused to let that small victory go unsupported.

'Why should I?' she challenged. 'You treat me like a child, and then don't like it when I retaliate——'

'—like a child,' he put in harshly. 'Where have you been, Martha? I want to know. I want to know where you were when Miss Powell arrived.'

Martha pursed her lips. 'I went for a walk. I'm sure you must have got that information from Sarah.'

'Information from your sister is invariably suspect,' he countered grimly. 'Where did you walk? Into the village? I would prefer it if you would refrain from behaving like one of the village girls, and acted instead in the manner to which they would expect my wife to be accustomed.' His gaze licked her contemptuously. 'And take your hair out of that ridiculous plait, before I tear it out by the roots!'

Martha quivered. 'Perhaps you'd prefer me to have it cut,' she suggested, remembering how in the old days he had insisted she should always keep it long, and his eyes narrowed ominously.

Leaving the door, he approached her on predator's feet, his mouth thin and dangerous, but the impulse to turn and escape from him was frozen by the anger in his eyes. She stood, motionless, while he went behind her, tearing the elastic band from her braid and dragging the strands free with reckless fingers. His careless action brought the tears to her eyes, but she didn't move, and presently he circled her again, to look down at her with warning insistence.

'Do not play games with me, Martha,' he told her coldly, holding her gaze with his own. 'And take off this ugly dress, too, and put on something more suited to your femininity.'

Martha's jaw stiffened. 'Perhaps you'd better choose that, as well,' she articulated, almost choking on the words, then gasped in horror when he took hold of the neckline of her dress and tore it half to her waist.

'Perhaps I had better,' he agreed savagely, turning aside from her to scan the garments laid out on the bed in readiness for hanging. 'This will do. Put this on. Or would you like me to dress you as well?'

'No——'

Martha clutched her torn bodice together with anxious fingers, and his expression revealed a bitter impatience. 'I have dressed you before,' he remarked, the silky lashes shading his eyes. 'And undressed you, too, if I remember correctly. I can act the lady's maid, when it is necessary, and get more—enjoyment out of it.'

Martha's breathing had quickened beneath the disturbing sensuality of his words. She had no doubts that Dion would do as he had threatened if she chose to oppose him again, and while her senses quickened at the prospect of his hands upon her body, her mind revolted from the images it created.

'Please, Dion ...' she whispered, despising herself for letting him abase her in this way, and with a careless shrug he gave the outfit he had chosen into her outstretched hand.

In the bathroom, she quickly removed the torn sundress, realising it was probably beyond repair. Then, after sluicing her face and arms beneath the taps, she stepped into the soft folds of the gown he had selected.

It was cream, a beautiful silky cream crêpe, with a classically draped bodice and a skirt that clung where it touched her flesh. There were no sleeves, but the shoulder draping of the bodice allowed folds of the material to brush her arms to the elbow, separating to reveal the honey-gold warmth of her skin. It was as well she didn't need a bra, she reflected, viewing herself with reluctant approval. The draping of the gown allowed for little in the way of undergarments.

She had expected him to be gone when she emerged from the bathroom, but Dion was still there, lounging against the dressing table, one foot raised to rest on the stool.

'*Maressi*,' he remarked, at her appearance, straightening

from his indolent position. 'I like it. Now, the hair. Would you like me to brush it for you?'

'I can manage,' retorted Martha, stepping jerkily towards the dressing table. 'You can go. I shan't do anything to spoil your creation.'

'I will decide when I choose to go,' he replied smoothly, lifting the brush and handing it to her. Then, as if compelled, he added: 'You are a beautiful woman, Martha. Why do you try so hard to hide it? You are not still afraid of me, are you?'

'Afraid? Of you?' Martha's mouth was dry as she tried to concentrate on her task. 'Don't be silly!'

'You think so?' he commented, moving behind her, and as her skin fairly prickled in expectation of his touch, he deliberately allowed his hand to slide under her arm to cup one rounded breast. She had to steel herself not to move as his fingers spread against the silky material, and the coolness of their touch was tangible against her over-heated flesh.

'I—wish you—wouldn't,' she got out at last, when the strain of holding herself motionless became almost unbearable, and his eyes met hers in the mirror.

'Why?' he challenged. 'I like touching you, I like feeling your reaction. And I have wasted too many years already, have I not?'

Martha's tongue appeared, almost involuntarily, circling her dry lips in trembling awareness of what he was doing to her, and with a muffled oath he released her, turning away towards the door, as if no longer willing to indulge in those kind of games.

'Come,' he said, impatience bringing an edge to his voice. 'Miss Powell is waiting to meet you.'

Martha hesitated only long enough to add a shiny lustre to her lips before accompanying him out of the room. Then they walked together the length of the corridor, emerging through a vine-hung archway on to the sunlit warmth of the patio.

Alex rose at their appearance, his dark eyes widening at the unexpected elegance of his sister-in-law. He had grown used to seeing her in shorts and jeans, and the cotton dresses she sometimes wore in the evenings, and Martha could see the youthful admiration deepening his regard.

But her eyes were searching for the nanny's, this woman Dion had employed to look after Josy, and when she found her, she experienced a certain amount of astonishment herself.

Miss Powell was nothing like Mrs Bennett, nor indeed typical of any nanny she had ever encountered. She was young, no more than twenty-two or three, with a slim attractive appearance, and curly dark hair. Her uniform was the only thing that set her apart from any other guest they might have entertained—a neat white blouse, and a suit of dark green linen, embroidered with the initials of the training establishment from which she had been recommended. She had a nice smile, too, showing a row of slightly uneven white teeth, and had it not been for Sarah's vaguely triumphant cynicism, Martha might well have liked her on sight.

The girl got to her feet, too, at their approach, and Josy, who had been sitting beside her, left her chair to come eagerly towards her mother.

'That's Miss Powell,' she announced, making the introduction without really being aware of it. 'Isn't she nice? She's been telling me I'm the first little girl she's ever taken care of.'

'Has she, darling?' Martha glanced half awkwardly at Dion, and taking control, he smoothly completely the exchange.

'This is—ah—Josy's mother,' he essayed easily, drawing Martha forward with a hand on her wrist, that only she knew was warning. 'She has been looking forward to meeting you.'

'Hello, Madame Myconos.'

Miss Powell held out her hand politely, and Martha was obliged to take it. They smiled at one another, though Martha's acknowledgement was a trifle forced, and then Dion released her and suggested they should all partake of the cold lunch Maria had prepared for them.

During the meal, it was easier to make an assessment of the other girl, and listening to her answering Dion's questions, Martha had to admit that she seemed genuinely fond of children. Josy, certainly, found her a fascinating addition to the household, and finding Sarah's eyes upon her, Martha had great difficulty in hiding her own uncertainty.

'I believe Mr Myconos told me that you are English, Madame Myconos,' Miss Powell ventured, spearing a dark-skinned olive into her mouth. 'Do you come from London, too?'

'Wimbledon,' Martha agreed, a trifle stiffly. 'I—er—do you?'

'Hampstead,' replied the other girl eagerly. 'But I'm looking forward to living in Greece. It's a wonderful climate, isn't it? And this island ...'

Her enthusiasm was eloquent, and Alex leaned forward to ask her whether she had ever visited the islands before.

'Well?' murmured Dion in Martha's ear, under cover of their conversation. 'What do you think?'

Martha looked down at her hands, clasped in her lap. 'I—she seems very nice,' she admitted in an undertone. 'She—she says she's looking forward to *living* in Greece. I gather she's here to stay.'

'But of course.' Dion deliberately covered both her hands with one of his, the familiarity holding an intimacy only Martha appreciated. 'This is a permanent arrangement,' he added. 'I thought you understood that.'

'Permanent?' Martha looked up at him uneasily. 'For whom?'

Dion's eyes narrowed. 'That is an unnecessary question,' he averred impatiently. 'Eat your lunch, and stop looking at me as if I was Satan incarnate!'

Martha removed her hands from their imprisonment and picked up her fork again. 'You always get your own way, don't you?' she demanded bitterly, and heard his weary intake of breath.

'If it pleases you to think so,' he replied, before turning to respond to Josy's tugging at his sleeve, and Martha was left to contend with Sarah's tight-lipped disapproval.

When lunch was over, Sophia appeared to show Miss Powell to her quarters, and after Josy had been forbidden to make a nuisance of herself, she accompanied them, leaving Martha feeling strangely deflated. Dion and Alex seemed engrossed in a conversation about oil production, and when Sarah excused herself to go to her room, Martha rose too.

However, Dion intervened. 'Where are you going?' he asked, transferring his attention from his brother to herself, and Sarah's rigid shoulders exhibited her opinion of his demand.

'I—I'm going to my room,' declared Martha, annoyed at the revealing tremor in her voice. 'Is that all right?'

'No, it is not all right,' retorted Dion, pushing back his chair. 'I want the company of my wife this afternoon, if that is not too much to ask of you.' His eyes flickered to Sarah's resentful features. 'But do not let us detain *you*!'

'You can't treat Martha like a slave, Dion,' Sarah asserted then, ignoring Martha's sigh of uneasiness. 'She's a person in her own right. You've got no control over her, other than through the child, and I think it's disgusting the way you're deliberately tormenting her!'

'Sarah ...'

Martha's plea was anxious, but Dion ignored it. 'I have not tormented her,' he contradicted coldly. 'I have not distorted her mind so that she no longer knows what to believe! But I do intend to change all that, and if you do not like it, then I regret you will just have to put up with it.'

'Martha!' Sarah stared at her sister now. 'Are you just going to stand there and let him speak to me any way he likes——'

'Dion——'

'Keep out of this affair, Martha.' His voice was taut with anger, and with a sound of fury Sarah swung her chair about and wheeled herself away without another word.

She was obviously offended, and Martha felt terrible. This was all her fault. But when she would have hurried after her sister, Dion moved swiftly, putting himself between them and facing his wife with hard intensity.

'Let her go,' he bit out violently. 'Believe me, I can be just as cruel as she can, and if you give me cause to do it, I can always send her away.'

Martha gasped, her mouth opening and shutting in speechless impotence, and with a groan of self-deprecation, he turned aside. 'Get your bathing suit,' he ordered, shrugging his shoulders at Alex, as if in apology for the scene he had just witnessed. 'We are leaving in five minutes. Do not keep me waiting.'

'And—and if I refuse?' Martha tendered, pressing her palms together in revealing agitation.

'Do not,' he advised, as he walked back to his brother, and returned to their conversation as if nothing untoward had happened.

Martha hesitated about going after Sarah, but she really did not have the time, and she was wary enough of Dion to know that he did not make idle threats. So instead she went to her own room, the room her husband had declared his intention to share, and was relieved to find that in her absence, the rest of her new wardrobe had been hung away.

She could not resist opening one of the wardrobe doors, however, but the sight of a row of jewel-bright dresses only reminded her that they were Dion's choice, not hers, and she quickly closed it again. Even so, she reflected, if he intended to take her swimming, and she rebelled at the implacability of his command, the dress she was presently wearing was hardly suitable for the beach, and ignoring the racks of pants and sweaters, she tugged out her old shorts and a faded pink vest, and discarded the cream crêpe across the bed.

Her only concession to his instructions was to leave her hair loose, and when she reappeared on the patio, she had the satisfaction of knowing he had not had it all his own way. Clutched in her hand was the navy bikini she had worn that morning, and although it was not wet, it was still a trifle damp as it clung to her fingers.

Dion was alone. Alex had apparently departed about some business of his own, and her husband viewed her indulgently from his position on a lounger before getting lazily to his feet to acknowledge her.

'Still the same old Martha,' he remarked, coming towards her and indicating the swimsuit in her hand. 'I am assured there were other swimming costumes in that collection of items I ordered from Hederakis,' he added, mentioning the name of a famous Greek fashion house. 'But no matter. What you wear is of little importance to me, as I intend we shall not be disturbed.'

Martha's nerves revealed themselves in the fluttering turmoil of her stomach, but she managed to hide her fears from Dion, and accompanied him through the gardens and across the courtyard to where an open-topped jeep was waiting.

The breeze soon brought disorder to her hair as they left the drive and circled the grounds of the villa, setting off across the island on the tussocky track more often used by sheep and goats. Yet it was exhilarating, feeling the wind tugging her hair from her scalp, and cooling the heated moistness at her nape. Dion's hair too was threaded into strands, falling thickly across his forehead as he turned his head to glance at her.

'We are going to Atvia,' he told her, referring to a tiny cove to the west of the island, protected by a rocky head-land, that forestalled any attempts at landing there. Martha had not been to the cove for more than seven years, not since long before their separation, the problems they were having precluding any romantic idylls, that could only end in argument.

She did not respond to him now, busy with her own thoughts, and he went on sharply: 'What is wrong? Does it bring back too many happy memories for you? Memories you would possibly rather forget!' and her nails dug into her palms at his obvious perception.

'I—I was thinking about Sarah, actually,' she lied, although her sister had not been far from her thoughts. 'You shouldn't treat her as you do. What has she ever done to you? Why should——'

'We will not speak of Sarah this afternoon,' Dion interrupted her harshly. 'I do not intend that this short time we have together should be poisoned by that woman's jealousy.'

'Jealousy!' Martha gasped. 'You're a fine one to talk about jealousy!'

'*Martha!*' His use of her name was driven from him. 'Please—I am appealing to you. Let us not speak of these things this afternoon. Can we not—simply enjoy the day? Is it impossible for us to be together without involving some other personality than our two selves?'

'I'm only saying ...' Martha began to speak, but then she closed her mouth again. What was the point of antagonising him? If they were to spend several hours in each other's company, wasn't it easier just to keep her own counsel? She could tell him what she really thought on their way home.

To get down to the cove it was necessary to leave the jeep and scramble down the scrubby face of the cliff. There were footholds, but its very inaccessibility made it more attractive. Dion went ahead, carrying a rucksack and some towels, and Martha came behind him, endeavouring not to require his proffered assistance.

The sand was bleached almost white by the sun, and warmed her curling toes as she surveyed the sheltered stretch of sea and shoreline. Only seabirds showed their disapproval at this intrusion, and the splashing sound of the water as it invaded the rock pools was a rhythmic background to their indignant cries.

Martha felt herself relaxing as the beauty of the place tore down her resentment, and when she found Dion watching her, she made him a little half rueful grimace. 'I'd forgotten what it was like,' she said, almost defensively, and he inclined his head in silent acquiescence.

Tossing down the towels and the rucksack, Dion walked to the water's edge, removing his sandals as he did so, allowing the rippling waves to curl around his toes. Martha watched him for a moment, and then, afraid of being observed in this activity, she squatted down on the sand, crossing her legs and unconsciously adopting a meditative pose.

When Dion turned back, he was unbuckling his belt, but although Martha stiffly concentrated at some point in the far distance, when he dropped his pants it was only to reveal a pair of blue cotton shorts. Then he removed his shirt before stretching his length beside her, the natural darkness of his skin requiring no protection from the undiluted rays of the sun.

Martha remained sitting in her cross-legged position, but gradually it became uncomfortable to maintain, and she longed to plunge herself into the blue-green water, and feel its softness washing away the sticky heat from her body.

Dion had closed his eyes when he lay down, and believing herself unobserved, she released the cotton vest from the waistband of her shorts. The slight coolness this engendered gave some relief, but not enough to make any appreciable difference to the prickly clamminess between her breasts.

'Why do you not take off your clothes?' Dion suggested softly, his words exploding the myth that he might be asleep. 'Put on your swimsuit, or swim without it. Whichever you do, there is no one to disturb us here.'

Martha drew an unsteady breath, smoothing her palms over her shapely knees. 'This—er—this bikini is still damp, from this morning,' she demurred. 'Besides, there's nowhere to change.'

Dion's response was a sigh of impatience. 'I will close my eyes, if it will make you feel any happier,' he essayed heavily. 'But do not imagine I do not remember exactly how you look without any clothes at all.'

Martha got abruptly to her feet, unable to sit still under such a disruptive statement, and Dion rolled on to his stomach, folding his arms beneath his head and turning his face aside. It was the nearest she was likely to come to complete privacy, and with fingers that stumbled over their task, she stripped off the vest and shorts and pulled on the briefs of the bikini. The bra was harder to manage. Dampness had distorted the elastic, and she was still struggling with the fastening when Dion rolled on to his back again.

His gaze swept up her, over the narrow feet and shapely calves, to the rounded promise of her thighs and the flat smoothness of her stomach. It was a deeply disturbing appraisal he subjected her to, and then, as his gaze moved higher, he perceived her difficulties, and got easily to his feet.

'Let me,' he said, turning her resisting body about, and taking the two sides of her bra from her. '*Eki*, it is done.

Tora, I suggest we swim for a little, so that you do not catch cold from putting on a wet costume, hmm——'

Martha pressed her lips together. 'Thanks,' she murmured, in belated gratitude for his fastening the bra, and with an offhand nod she indicated that she was willing to fall in with his plans.

The water felt cold at first, and she could not repress the squeal of excitement that escaped her when the first wave lapped about her hips and thighs. Dion grinned and dived into the succeeding breakers, but Martha met it head on, gasping in the spray, and finding herself forced to take her feet from the sandy bottom and swim into calmer waters. As her blood cooled with the temperature of the water, she realised how warm it really was, refreshingly vital against her stimulated flesh.

Dion swam back to her, circling her with lazy strokes, and she turned on to her back to float to avoid his mocking eyes. But a hand on her midriff propelled her downwards, and she came up spluttering to find him laughing at her confusion. She was angry as she swam after him, though when she caught him she knew he had let her, and her indignation gave way to amusement as she fought to duck him as he had done to her.

'You are not strong enough,' he teased, fending off her attacks without much effort. 'See, I will go under, if that is what you wish——' and he dived down beneath her, terrifying her by swimming between her legs and bringing her up gasping on his shoulders.

'Dion!' she squealed, forgetting altogether the prelude to this outing, and he obediently did a backward somersault into the water, allowing her to scramble free of him once again.

Martha discovered she was enjoying herself tremendously. It was years since anyone had played with her like this, indeed, only Dion had ever done so, and a wave of nostalgia swept over her for those days before all the rows and recriminations had raised their ugly heads.

Later, they stretched out on the sand on towels, side by side, curiously at peace, Martha realised, despite their obvious differences. But lying there, she knew an almost overwhelming temptation to induce the kind of scene they had had in the bedroom the previous evening, and she had to actually steel herself from reaching out and touching him.

'Tell me,' Dion said suddenly, shading his eyes with a lazy arm, 'would you ever have told me about Josy, if this situation with Scott had not arisen?'

Martha sighed, loath to spoil the harmony between them. 'I don't know,' she answered honestly. 'I would like to think so. But after seeing you again ...'

'Yes?' Dion rolled on to his side, propping himself up on one elbow. 'What then?'

Martha shook her head helplessly. 'You—you seemed so—so hard, so implacable! When you—when you made me tell you, I—I think I hated you then.'

Dion's mouth twisted. 'Go on.'

Martha glanced sideways at him. 'What more is there to say? You know what happened next. You came to England, and after you'd seen Josy, you knew!'

'No,' Dion made a negative gesture, 'I do not mean that. I mean—tell me why you like to think you would have told me yourself, without any inducement. I want to know.'

'Oh ...' Martha moved her shoulders uneasily. 'Because of Josy, I suppose. I mean, I knew it wasn't fair to her not —not telling you.'

'And that is all?' Dion's eyes narrowed.

'What—what else could there be?'

'You might have wanted to show me what a beautiful child we had made together,' he suggested huskily, and her senses quivered in awareness of his devastating attraction.

'After—after what you had said?' she ventured, and his eyes darkened in impatience.

'*Mou theos*, Martha, you can have no conception of

what it feels like to believe that the woman you love—the woman you *worship*—has lain with another man!' His face twisted in remembered bitterness. 'I wanted to hurt you, as you had hurt me, but worse—much worse, and there was nothing I could do! So I said things, unforgivable things, I admit, but I believed them at that time. That is my only excuse!'

Trembling, Martha sat up, wrapping her arms around her drawn-up knees, and staring out blindly towards the headland. So there was no mistake. He *had* believed the worst of her. How could he talk of love, of worship, when there was no trust? That was not love, it was desire, as she had known all along. Did he expect her to condone it now—now that he had taken her back?

'Martha ...' He had sat up, too, and was regarding her with those liquid dark eyes, eyes that could drag the very soul out of her, and bare it to his uncaring domination. 'Is it impossible for you to understand how I was feeling? Is there no shred of compassion in your heart for someone who has gone through five years of hell since you left him?'

Martha's emotions were scarcely proof against such a blatant assault, and unwilling to pursue such a volatile subject, she said, somewhat unsteadily:

'Five years is a long time for anyone to wait, Dion. I find your—your declaration of suffering hard to believe after—after all this time.'

His oath was in his own language, but none the less savage because of that. '*Hristo*, Martha, what did you expect me to do, when—when——'

'When what?' she asked, puzzled by the look of anguish that crossed his face as he broke off what he was saying, and he turned his head away, massaging the back of his neck with a violence that mirrored his agitation.

There was silence for several minutes, and then he expelled his breath on a sigh, turning back to her wearily. 'You are never going to believe me, are you?' he demanded harshly. 'You will always blame me for what has happened.'

Martha bent her head, disturbed in spite of herself by the look in his eyes. 'Dion ... she began unhappily, but then faltered into silence when his hand came to grip her neck, just below the ear, turning her face towards him.

'Tell me you do not want me to do this, and I will stop,' he said roughly, his tongue stroking the outline of her mouth, and almost involuntarily her lips parted. 'So tender —it is like kissing the virgin you were when first I made love to you,' he added hoarsely. '*Theos*, little one, do you remember how it was then?'

Martha remembered. How could she forget, with his lips coaxing her instinctive response to his invasion, his mouth searching the parted contours of hers, as if eager to taste every inch of its moist sweetness. With her lungs quickening in breathless haste, her hand touched Dion's shoulder almost tentatively, responding to its cool masculinity by digging her nails into his flesh. Then, as he pressed her back against the towel, his hand freed the clip he had earlier fastened, and his hair-roughened chest rubbed sensuously against the hardening nipples of her breasts.

He lay half over her, one of his legs imprisoning both of hers, his hands moving intimately over her, invading the secret places of her body. She had no will to resist him as his mouth performed its own exploration, returning again and again to hers, drugging her with long demanding kisses.

Her hands were smooth against his shoulders, eagerly stroking his muscular flesh, inspiring sensations she had thought she no longer possessed. The hair at the nape of his neck was virile to her touch, and the powerful strength of his body aroused an answering need in her own. She wanted him, she thought helplessly, she needed him to satisfy this ache that was growing inside her, and no matter what came after, she would not prevent him from taking what was undeniably his.

'Is good?' he muttered, biting her ear-lobe, his English suffering at the hands of his emotions, and Martha arched her body provocatively under his, nodding eagerly, as she whispered: 'You know it is,' in urgent husky tones. 'Oh, Dion, there's never been anyone else but you ...'

'I know that now,' he assured her passionately, and although Martha heard his words in pained denigration, she could not stifle the desires that were shredding her resistance, making a mockery of her will to deny him.

She was bereft when he suddenly rolled away from her, turning on to his back and gazing up into the heavens with tightly controlled features. She couldn't believe he had left her, that he had actually repulsed her once again, and for several minutes she could not move, torn by the pain of emotions aroused and not satisfied. He couldn't do this to her, she thought disbelievingly, nor to himself. But the fact remained that he had, and the merciless awareness of rejection swept over her.

That brought her to puppet-like life. Jerkily she sat up, groping for the bra of the bikini and fastening it now without any of the effort she had experienced earlier. It was silly really, she thought, trying to restore some measure of reality. Maybe the fact that her fingers were trembling so badly accounted for their accuracy. At any rate, with the bra in place, she felt less vulnerable to his contempt, for she could think of no other reason for his incomprehensible behaviour.

As if becoming aware of her movements, Dion moved now, pushing himself up on to his haunches, squatting before her with curiously angry eyes.

'What of your resentment now, my love?' he demanded harshly. 'Exactly what kind of a man do you think I am?'

'I—I don't know what you mean——'

'Oh, I think you do.' His lips twisted. 'I am not a fool. You want me—I know that. And God alone knows, I cannot disguise my own desire. But how long will it last, that is what I ask myself. When the doubts return? I can arouse your emotions, but can I arouse your heart? You do me an injustice, if you think I want only your body. That is not the way of my family.'

'To—total possession, is that what you mean?' Martha faltered tremulously. 'And—and can you deny you only want me because—because of Josy?'

'*Josy!*' He glared at her so savagely that she shrank away from him. 'You can speak of Josy at a time like this?' With a discarded gesture, he got to his feet. 'Put on your clothes,' he said wearily. 'Cover yourself! We have nothing more to say to one another!'

CHAPTER NINE

THE Myconos villa in Athens was a far more formal residence than the casual luxury of the villa on Mycos. For one thing, there was not the freedom to come and go at will, the easy familiarity between servant and master that existed far from the seat of power. The bodyguards that patrolled the main entrance and the grounds were all too real and necessary, and despite the lived-in atmosphere of the family apartments, most of the rooms at the villa were chillingly impersonal.

Preparing for dinner in the bedroom she was supposed to share with Dion, Martha felt the weight of her own uncertainties bearing down upon her. She felt nervous and uneasy, and terribly confused, and her husband's attitude towards her in no way relieved her burden.

She supposed she ought to feel glad that he had refrained from tormenting her, from touching her or mocking her, or doing anything to discompose her carefully erected façade of confidence, but she wasn't. She was torn between the knowledge that he expected more of her than he could conceivably demand, and the growing awareness that his detached impartiality was the purest kind of torture.

Not that he was unkind to her. On the contrary, since that scene at Atvia more than a week ago he had behaved with the utmost circumspection, treating her with polite deference in the company of others, and total indifference when they were alone.

Leaving Mycos had not been the ordeal Martha had expected. Josy's reactions to Miss Powell—or Jill, as she pre-

ferred to be called—had made life easier for her, and her
fears about her daughter's loyalties had proved groundless.
Jill was a thoroughly nice girl, but she was only twenty-
two, and far more interested in Alex than in stealing the
affections of a five-year-old. She did her job, and the little
girl liked her, but the novelty of having someone constantly
available to supervise her had soon worn off, and Josy had
reverted to asking her mother to read her stories, and plaguing both Dion and Alex to play with her in the pool.

Nevertheless, it had been simpler to leave her on Mycos
in Jill's charge, Martha had to admit, although Sarah had
not refrained from voicing her biased opinions. Her continuing bitterness left a sour taste in Martha's mouth, and
she wondered if she was truly as gullible as Sarah would
have her believe.

The night before she left Mycos she had voiced some of
these doubts to Roger, but he had only scoffed at her
anxieties. 'Sarah likes to complain, haven't you noticed?'
he exclaimed, breaking off the stem of a camellia and inhal-
ing its delicate fragrance. 'I don't know, maybe she was
always like this. Maybe we just didn't notice it before.'

Martha shook her head, tilting it backwards so that she
could look up at the arc of the night sky above them. Velvet-
soft, and studded with stars, it had a jewel-like brilliance,
and she wondered how her sister could view so much
beauty with so little pleasure.

'What else could I do, Roger?' she asked rather helplessly now. 'Dion——'

'Stop blaming yourself!' declared Roger impatiently. 'It
had to happen sooner or later, I could see that. As Josy
grew older, you were bound to have doubts.'

'Doubts?'

'Yes, doubts.' Roger's sigh was exasperated. 'You know
I'm right, so why don't you admit it? I saw how you reacted, every time the child's parentage was questioned. You
were eaten up with guilt, and you know it.'

Martha sighed. 'So you think I was right to—to tell him?'

'Of course. Don't you? Honestly?'

Now Martha touched the strand of silky hair that trailed effectively over one shoulder. She had not really given Roger an answer, but her expression had said it for her. Dear Roger, she thought regretfully. If only she had fallen in love with someone like him, someone she liked and understood, instead of a volatile Greek, with all the pride and arrogance of his race.

Coming to Athens, to the Myconos villa, had been a nerve-racking experience. Athens was sweltering in the midsummer heat, but these halls and apartments were air-conditioned, and Dion's parents had greeted her as coolly as their surroundings allowed. Not that she could entirely blame them. Naturally, they only saw the situation from Dion's viewpoint, and obviously they had been hoping that he was about to break this connection which had caused them so much distress.

Someone else had greeted her coolly, too. The woman who, according to the little maid who had been assigned to look after her, had been hoping to become the next Madame Myconos. Julia Kuriakin, whom she had met on her first night in Athens, and who had made it patently clear that she saw Martha's intervention as only a temporary setback. She had treated Dion with an annoying familiarity, that spoke of the closeness of their association, and Martha had spent the entire evening fretting with emotions she had imagined were his sole prerogative.

Maybe Julia was right, she thought now, touching a delicate perfume to her neck and wrists. Maybe Dion had had his own motives for behaving as he had. Had she imagined his ardour down on the beach? Had his intention been to seduce her, and her involuntary response thwarted him? She did not know. She did not even understand why he had got so angry with her. But what was becoming painfully evident was that she could not live with Dion in this state of bland neutrality.

She shook her head, and the curtain of her hair swung softly against her cheek. Could she forgive him? she asked herself helplessly, the bruised darkness of sleepless nights shadowing her eyes. Was that what she really wanted? Was it what *he* wanted? And if not, how could she, even for Josy's sake, prolong this agony of aching emptiness? Even the half life she had had with him before was better than nothing, though her mind rebelled from the weeks and months of separation she had been expected to bear.

The door to Dion's dressing room opened to admit the man whose nearness promoted an increasing anguish. In a dark grey velvet dinner suit, he was disturbingly attractive, the fine texture of the cloth only accentuating his rugged maleness. Martha's eyes were drawn to him like a magnet, lingering on the muscular width of his shoulders, the powerful strength of his legs.

The dressing room was also the place where he had slept since they came to Athens, much to the whispered speculation of the servants, she was sure. However, he seemed unconcerned that there might be any conjecture about them, behaving as if it was the most natural thing in the world that they should have separate rooms. She was waiting in nervous anticipation for the information to come to the ears of his parents, for she was sure when that happened, her position here would become completely intolerable.

'Are you ready?' Dion enquired now, coming into the room and closing the dressing room door behind him. 'I see you took my advice about what to wear. I am glad. The colour suits you.'

'Thank you.'

Martha endeavoured to keep her voice as expressionless as his as she rose from her seat at the vanity unit. She could not help but see that the rich, wine-coloured silk did wonders for her creamily-tanned flesh, its draped skirt hinting at the length of leg visible between each of the floating panels. The bodice was low and simple, two boot-lace straps tied in provocative knots above the rounded smoothness of her shoulders, while a narrow waistline accentuated the swaying maturity of her hips. Irene, the little maid who attended her, had delivered the message that Kirios Dionysus wished her to wear this particular gown this evening, and because the prospect of this party was already quite intimidating, she had had no hesitation in obeying his instructions. Besides, the gown was beautiful, and she wanted to look her best.

'I have something here which might be a suitable addition,' Dion remarked now, crossing the floor to stand behind her, removing a narrow case from his inside pocket. 'Take it,' he said, handing it to her, and she caught her breath at the necklace and earrings that lay on its white velvet lining.

'I—I don't know what to say,' she murmured, her throat closing up with the intensity of her feelings. 'They're beautiful. But not for me, surely?'

'Rubies and diamonds,' remarked Dion, without emotion. 'An ideal combination with what you are wearing. Here, let me fasten it for you.'

Martha stood quite still as he clipped the necklace at her nape, and then covered the cold stones with her fingers as they chilled her throat. This was obviously why he had asked her to wear the gown, and she wondered when he had purchased such an expensive trinket.

'Now—the earrings,' he suggested, offering them to her. 'Can you fasten them yourself? *Kalos*. You look every inch the pampered wife, no?'

Martha pressed her lips together, staring at her reflection without enthusiasm. 'Is that why you bought them?' she asked, her voice low and uneven. 'So that I wouldn't let you down in front of all your friends? So no one could say that Dionysus Myconos is not generous to his wife, no matter how shameful her behaviour has been?'

'I bought them because I did not think you would wish to wear the jewels you left behind you when you walked out on me!' he stated grimly, showing the first traces of emotion she had seen for days. 'Now, if you are ready, shall we go? My parents, and Nikos and Cassandra, are already waiting for us.'

Martha collected a gauzy wrap, and without another word, preceded him out of the room. Obviously, her appearance had made no impression on him, and it was hardly an auspicious beginning to what promised to be another nerve-racking ordeal.

The party was being held on board Andrea Stangos's yacht, moored off Mikrolimano, near the picturesque harbour where the Hellenic Yacht Club had its headquarters. Like all these occasions, it was an opportunity for the men to talk business in more relaxed surroundings, while their wives circulated together, picking up the latest gossip. Martha had attended many such functions when she and Dion had first lived together, but tonight she was on edge and uneasy, aware that her own attendance would be a primary source of speculation. When she had attempted to protest at Dion's reasons for bringing her, he had refused to discuss it, stating merely that the sooner their friends became aware of their reconciliation the better. Martha did not agree. These people were Dion's friends, not hers, and being put on display as it were, for their benefit, could only embarrass her. However, he was adamant, and she wondered exactly how long he expected her unquestioning obedience.

They drove to Mikrolimano in a chauffeured limousine, a long black snake of a car, with two rows of luxuriously upholstered seats behind that containing the driver. Martha found herself in the rear seat, between her mother-in-law and Cassandra, Nikos's wife, while the three men occupied the seat in front. It was the usual start to the evening, the

separation of the sexes beginning early, and Martha's head
began to ache a little at the prospect of meeting all the other
wives, by whom she had obviously been condemned.

'And how is little Sandro this evening?' Madame Myconos enquired now, speaking across Martha to her other
daughter-in-law. She spoke in Greek, but Martha did not
find it difficult to understand her, her own familiarity with
the language returning with every passing day.

Cassandra, who was dark and plump and very Greek,
gave her mother-in-law a gentle smile. 'He is much better,
Mama, thank you,' she answered with evident satisfaction.
'The spots are almost gone now, and only a little irritation
remains.'

'That is good.' Ariadne Myconos nodded her greying
head, and Martha felt herself stiffening as the dark, piercing
gaze was turned in her direction. 'And I suppose we will
eventually get to meet our other granddaughter,' she remarked coldly. 'Although I agree, after five years, what is
a week more or less?'

As Martha strove for words to answer her, Dion turned
in his seat in front of his mother, and rested his arm along
the back. 'You know the situation, Mama,' he advised her
steadily. 'I told you—Josy has not yet had time to adapt to
her new surroundings. It would have been foolish to uproot
her once again to bring her to Athens, when it is so hot,
and your visit to Mycos is only a few days away.'

This was the first Martha had heard of this, and her eyes
sought her husband's for explanation. But he had already
turned round again to answer some question posed by his
father, and Ariadne acknowledged his explanation with a
little dismissing flutter of her hands.

'We are all looking forward to meeting—Josy,' said Cassandra kindly, bestowing her smile on the other girl. She
was about Martha's own age, but very different in personality, asking nothing more of her husband's life than the
minute portion he chose to give her. She already had three

children, Alessandro, the eldest, being about Josy's age.

'*Josy!*' declared her mother-in-law disparagingly. 'Whoever chose such a name for the child? She should have been called Louise or Cristina.'

'My mother's name was Josephine,' Martha replied quietly, and the older woman subsided into a disagreeable silence as Cassandra chose to speak again.

'She is five, is she not?' she asked, obviously interested. 'Sandro is five, too. They will be playmates for one another.'

'Yes.' Martha was a little awkward, but ignoring her mother-in-law's disapproval, she added: 'Has—Sandro been ill? I couldn't help listening to what you were saying. Rashes must be so unpleasant in this heat.'

Cassandra nodded. 'It was the measles,' she explained, pulling a face. 'Poor Sandro! He was quite poorly. Happily now, though, he is recovered, and looking forward to coming to Mycos.'

Martha managed to conceal her alarm at the prospective advent of so many visitors. Was she expected to entertain them all? Would Alex be there? Or was this to be another of those occasions when the male members of the household departed about their business, leaving their wives to look after the children? It had happened before. Would she feel differently now that she had a child of her own? From Josy's point of view, it was the best thing that could happen to her, mixing with other children who were also her cousins. She would have a whale of a time, and with Jill Powell to look after her, she would need no one else. Not even her mother ...

The Stangos yacht was a blaze of coloured lights, a glowing beacon of music and conversation. There was plenty of food, plenty to drink, and dancing for those energetic enough to take advantage of the specially sprung deck. Martha thought it was more like a cruise liner than anyone's private sailing craft, but at least it would be easy to find anonymity among so many other guests.

Andrea Stangos was a short, stocky individual, a business colleague of the family, whom Martha did recall meeting once several years ago. His wife resembled him, though the formality of his white dinner jacket could not compete with the rings and bracelets that occupied every vacant inch of her flesh. Obviously she enjoyed displaying the fruits of his labours, though for someone who was reputed to earn a certain number of dollars every time he took a breath, Martha did not think he looked overworked.

Her arrival was greeted with mixed feelings. Everyone was incredibly polite, but she sensed the vaguely malicious speculation that went on behind casually concealing hands, and wondered how Dion could appear so indifferent to their mildly outraged indignation.

After the initial introductions were over, and everyone seemed absorbed in conversation, Martha took the opportunity to slip away unnoticed. The last thing she wanted was to become the cynosure of a group of enquiring females, and she wished it was possible for her to disappear completely until the evening was over.

Leaning on the rail at the far end of the yacht, she watched the play of lights in the water. It was a beautiful evening, the heat of the day mellowed to a peachy softness, darkness lapping about her like a velvet cloak. Nowhere were the nights more delightful than in these southern waters, and she sighed when she thought of the artificiality of the party going on without her.

'Champagne?' enquired a husky voice behind her, and she started in alarm. Her consternation did not ease when she recognised her husband, and she took the slim glass from his hand with evident reluctance. 'What do you think you are doing?' he continued, after swallowing a mouthful of his champagne. 'I did not bring you here to lurk about in the shadows, hoping no one will notice your absence until it is time to leave.'

'How well you know me,' murmured Martha, rather tremulously, sipping from her own glass. 'Why did you bring me here, Dion? To humiliate me? To embarrass me? Or just to demonstrate your mastery over me?'

Dion sighed now, resting his arms on the rail beside her, and staring out to sea with a distant expression. 'Would you believe—for none of those reasons?' he demanded flatly. 'We are man and wife again, Martha. I see no reason to hide that fact.'

Martha made no response to this, and half impatiently, he turned to look at her. 'Well?' he said. 'Shall we return to the other guests? Or do you wish them to speculate precisely what we might be doing in this most secluded part of the ship?'

Martha held up her head. 'You go back to—to the party,' she said. 'I would rather stay here. It—it's quiet. And I have a headache.'

'Do you?' His expression was sceptical. 'How convenient!'

'It's not, actually,' Martha defended herself. 'It's rather inconvenient. Besides,' she hesitated before continuing, 'you know if I go back there, I'll become the—the brunt of all the resentment they feel at your audacity in bringing me here!'

'Is that what you think?' he drawled, his dark brows drawing together. 'You think I brought you here to abandon you, is that it?'

'And didn't you? Haven't you always?'

Dion's mouth twisted with bitter humour. 'In the past, maybe,' he conceded. 'Before I learned better.'

'What do you mean?'

'Come,' he said, putting his fingers round her upper arm. 'I shall not—abandon you. Not tonight. Not ever.'

Martha's grey eyes widened at this declaration, but Dion was already propelling her along the deck. He made these statements without giving any real thought to their outcome, she thought despairingly, and she, for one, could not go on living in ambiguity.

With Dion at her side, the stalwart matrons and their younger counterparts had to accept Martha as one of their number. Apart from his obvious influence with their husbands, he was a popular man, and much of the animosity exhibited towards his wife was the result of jealousy. She was the only English girl among their number, and the disapproval that had briefly been silenced by their marriage had quickly resurrected itself when she had behaved so outrageously. The fact that they appeared to have mended their differences was therefore hard to swallow, and time alone would convince them that Dion was not making another mistake in taking her back. So far as the child was concerned, she would be judged on her own merits, and Martha hoped that Josy would never feel as alien as she did tonight.

She had not noticed Julia Kuriakin's presence earlier, but now the Greek girl detached herself from her escort and made her way to where Dion and Martha were exchanging small talk with a Greek politician and his wife.

'My dear!' she exclaimed, addressing Dion in their own language, as she always did. 'I thought you had not yet arrived. I was speaking to your mother and father a few moments ago, but they omitted to tell me that you and—er —your wife—were here.'

'We came together,' replied Dion smoothly, his hand at Martha's waist, preventing her from moving away from him. 'You know Doctor and Madame Spirodon, do you not? We were just deploring the temperatures in the city this afternoon.'

'Oh, yes.' Julia's thin smile encompassed the other members of the group, before returning avidly to the younger man's face. 'I looked for you at the Academy this morning, Dion,' she added guilefully, 'but apparently my little exhibition slipped your mind for some reason.'

Her gaze flicked his wife contemptuously, and Martha could feel the warmth of indignation sweeping up her cheeks. So Dion was not above making assignations with some other woman, even while she was in Athens. What price now his hollow talk of reconciliation?

With the Spirodons looking on in somewhat embarrassed silence, Dion smote his forehead with an impatient palm.

'*Theos!*' he exclaimed. 'Prato's exhibition! I apologise. We did forget all about it.'

We?

While Martha struggled with a mingled sense of relief and resentment, Julia's expression could not entirely conceal the irritation his statement had evoked. However, controlling her feelings, she managed to say gracefully: 'No doubt you have other things on your mind at the moment, my dear,' and looked at Martha again, as if daring her to deny it.

'Indeed.' Dion inclined his head now, and only Martha was aware that his arm about her waist had tightened. 'I am especially sorry because my wife would have enjoyed seeing your friend's paintings, I am sure. I did tell you Julia was something of a patron of the arts—and the artists, did I not, darling?'

Martha quivered beneath that deliberate endearment, but when she turned her head sharply to meet his gaze, she was disconcerted by the warmth of his appraisal. It was all very well telling herself that he was only acting this way to convince the Spirodons of their affection for one another, to allay the suspicions of any of the guests present, that in any case, he had never mentioned Julia's exhibition to her, but when he looked at her like that, she felt incapable of defying him.

'I—well—yes,' she got out at last, jerking her head round to face Julia. 'It sounds a—a fascinating hobby. Perhaps we could arrange to come at some other time.'

'I think not.' Julia's expression was unguarded now and

the angry resentment was there for all to see. 'It seems your current responsibilities leave you little time for enjoyment, Dion,' she stated contemptuously. 'Perhaps you had better contact me again when you are not so—heavily committed.'

The insult was unmistakable, and Martha's embarrassment was complete. She had no idea of Dion's commitment towards this woman, but whatever it was, she refused to stand by and be abused in front of him and anyone who might be listening. With a stiffening of her spine she opened her mouth to defend herself, then closed it again when Dion began to speak.

'I doubt if you and I will have anything further to say to one another after tonight, Julia,' he remarked, the mildness of his tone belying the cold incision of his words. 'It appears you are suffering some misconception regarding my feelings towards you. I am sorry.' A half smile made a mockery of his apology. 'Surely you were always aware of the fact that I was married. I have a wife ...' he glanced briefly at Martha's shocked face, '... and a daughter. And although I find you an attractive young woman, I have no need of a mistress.'

It was harsh and it was cruel, and Martha could find it in her heart to feel sorry for the other girl. She even shivered as Julia made some futile word of apology to the Spirodons, before disappearing into the throng surrounding the buffet tables, but she knew that given the opportunity, Julia would not have pitied her.

'*Eki*, I, too, am sorry,' Dion apologised courteously, keeping his hold on Martha. 'And now, if you will excuse us ...' And he drew his wife on to the apron-sized dance floor.

Martha had no time to protest, before he had drawn her close to him, enfolding her in the circle of his arms, with all the self-assurance of a lover. The music was low and melodic, and she felt the shudder that shook his body as she relaxed against him and allowed the tempo of the rhythm to dictate her movements. The last few minutes had been exhausting ones for both of them, she suspected, and while there were things she wanted to ask, for the moment she was too weak to resist him.

'Thank you,' he said at last, turning his face into her nape, and allowing his lips to move against her skin.

'For—for what?' she probed, her cheek against his shoulder. 'Not exposing you for the fraud you are?'

'Fraud?' he echoed huskily. 'I am no fraud.'

'But you did not tell me about Julia's exhibition,' she pointed out.

'No, I did not do that,' he agreed huskily. 'But equally, I did not encourage her to run after me.'

'So you admit she did?'

'I cannot believe you are jealous,' he remarked dryly, drawing back slightly to look down at her. 'As I recall, that word occupies no place in your vocabulary.'

'You're right.' Martha endeavoured to keep her tone light. 'Nevertheless, you haven't answered my question.'

'All right.' Dion moved his shoulders in weary acquiescence. 'There have been one or two women who perhaps fancied the idea of becoming the next Madame Myconos. Those jewels around your neck alone would inspire the most ardent declarations of love from certain members of your sex.'

Martha's smile was tight. 'You underestimate yourself, Dion. Even without the jewels, you're quite a prize.'

'Do you think so?' His eyes were intent.

'We're not discussing me,' she retorted carefully. 'But once I would have said yes.'

'Once?' His mouth twisted. 'You are so romantic, *mou kardhia*.'

Martha bent her head. 'How soon can we leave? Now that you have proved I can be manipulated, can we go home?'

'Home?' he mocked. 'Dare I believe that like Josy, you are beginning to regard this place as your home?'

Martha avoided his eyes. 'Don't bait me, Dion,' she begged, tightly, and with a muffled profanity he released her.

In the event, they did leave before the others. Martha's headache had become a throbbing reality, and when Dion discovered that some friends of his were leaving at eleven, he suggested they accept the lift they offered. If their departure was looked on with disapproval by his parents, Dion did not seem to care, and Martha relaxed in the back of the Stephanoses' saloon with some relief. Paul Stephanos was the editor of a newspaper here in Athens, and his wife was heavily pregnant. She seemed drowsy, and consequently Martha was not obliged to make conversation on the journey back to the city.

The villa seemed strangely empty without the presence of Aristotle and Ariadne, and crossing the marble-tiled entrance hall, Martha felt a sense of relief that they had returned alone. The usual post-mortem on the proceedings that her mother-in-law liked to conduct would not now take place, and she was free to go to bed without offering any excuse. Even her headache was receding in the coolness of the air-conditioning, though her sigh of satisfaction was misinterpreted by her husband.

'Go to bed,' he said wearily, walking into the ornate beauty of the main salon. 'I need a drink, then I too intend to retire. We will be returning to Mycos tomorrow, but do not put away your suitcases. I will be leaving for New York in a matter of ten days or so.'

'New York!' Martha halted, with one hand on the marble balustrade. 'But I——'

'You will be accompanying me,' he stated, his expression guarded. 'Did I not make myself clear? That is why I have hired a suitable nursemaid. I should not like Josy to suffer for my actions.'

Martha licked her lips bewilderedly, and with a shrug he left her, disappearing into the salon and leaving her to ponder this entirely unexpected development. He was taking her with him to New York, she acknowledged incredulously. He intended to extend their unnatural relationship into areas previously barred to her. Was this his revenge, his method of punishing her—or had he motives even she could not identify?

In the bedroom the lamp was lit beside the bed, its copper shade casting a mellow radiance over dark wood and rich silk draperies. The predominating colour in the room was cinnamon, shading from palest beige to deepest amber, with shades of gold and topaz in between. The bed was huge and opulent, the damask coverlet turned back to display sheets of rich brown silk, and pillows edged with coffee-coloured lace, while the carpet underfoot was honey-gold, and softly luxurious.

Shedding her wrap, Martha kicked off her high-heeled sandals, removed her jewellery and walked disconsolately across the floor. Now that she was alone at last she did not care for the situation, and the turmoil of her thoughts left little room for relaxation. What was Dion trying to do to her? she asked herself perplexedly, her brow furrowing in her confusion. What possible use could he have for her in New York, except as a target on which to vent his spleen? Hadn't he proved his point by taking her to the party tonight, without forcing her to repeat the humiliation in every other capital of the world?

She sat down on the bed and peeled off her tights, anxiety dilating the pupils of her eyes. This couldn't go on, she told herself fiercely; no matter what was at stake, the break would have to come. It wasn't just his present attitude towards her, which was hard enough to bear, goodness knows. It was the way he was making her feel about him, and the realisation that his behaviour towards her at the time of Josy's birth was gradually becoming less important than the desperate need he inspired inside her.

Getting up from the bed again, she unfastened the straps

at the shoulders of her gown and allowed it to fall unheeded to the floor at her feet. She had given Irene the night off, half embarrassed on those occasions when the girl had waited up to attend to her toilette, and stepping out of the folds she walked into the bathroom.

The bathroom matched the bedroom, its porcelain tiles shading from cream to gold, the huge sunken bath capable of accommodating half a dozen people. Martha found it rather intimidating, but she could not deny a certain admiration for its magnificence.

Hesitating now, she looked at the bath again, and on impulse bent to turn on the taps. Since her arrival seven days ago she had invariably used the shower, but the temptation to submerge herself in scented water was heightened at the realisation that it might possibly help her to sleep.

She added some of the contents of a jar of bath salts she found in the cabinet to the water, and felt a reluctant smile tugging at her lips as the water foamed and bubbled around the rim. It was tantalising stepping into its soapy depths, and she sank down luxuriously, uncaring that the ends of her hair were getting wet.

The warmth was narcotic, and her eyelids drooped after a time, and she drowsed. It was so pleasant, relaxing in the steamy atmosphere, and she forgot all about the party, and Julia's unpleasantness, and remembered only the feel of Dion's body as he had moved with her around the tiny dance floor.

'Martha! Martha, what are you doing in there?'

Her husband's voice seemed to reach her from a far distance, and she opened her eyes reluctantly to the realisation that he was knocking on the bathroom door.

'Martha! Answer me!' There was concern in his voice now, as he repeated his command. 'What is the matter?'

Martha wriggled into a more comfortable position, and then called back: 'I'm all right. I'm taking a bath. I—you—you can come in, if you want to. The door's not locked.'

Dion needed no second bidding, and he entered the room abruptly, his expression dark with irritation. She saw at once why he had been so impatient, her eyes acknowledging his bare feet and carelessly tied robe, and guessed that he, too, had intended to take advantage of the bath.

'Do you realise you have been in here over half an hour?' he demanded, standing over her impatiently. 'I thought something must have happened to you, taking so long. I did not realise you had been taking a nap!'

Martha shifted lazily. 'Does it matter? I'm sorry if you've been waiting to use the bathroom——'

'I have not been waiting to use the bathroom,' he snapped, shortly. 'There are plenty of other bathrooms, without using this one. But I must admit, I have not used them, simply because I was concerned about you!'

'Well, I'm sorry.' Martha shuffled into a sitting position, aware as she did so that the upper half of her body was now revealed to his angry gaze, rose-tipped and deliciously soapy. 'You should have knocked sooner. I didn't think you would notice. You said you were going to have a drink.'

'A drink!' he agreed. 'Not a whole bottle.' His hands balled at his sides. 'At first I thought you must be elsewhere, but when I discovered you were not, I thought of the bathroom.' He gestured towards her impatiently. 'Cover yourself up, can you not?'

'Is that what you want me to do?' she asked, still bemused from her sudden awakening, and tantalised by his nearness. 'Were you going to take a bath, Dion? Is that why you are wearing this?' Her fingers reached out and touched his bathrobe.

'What I was about to do is not important,' he retorted harshly, his expression revealing his irritation. 'I suggest you get out before the water cools completely.'

'Oh, but it's quite refreshing,' Martha taunted, enjoying his discomposure. 'I had a shower before I went out, but I thought a bath might relax me—and it has.'

'Martha!' The word was anguished. 'In the name of all the saints, what are you trying to do to me?'

'What am *I* trying to do to *you*?' she echoed, as if not understanding him. 'Why, nothing. I'm only taking a bath. I'm sorry if the sight of my body offends you.'

He turned away at that, his shoulders stiff with some emotion he was desperately trying to suppress, and she could not bear it any longer. 'Dion!' she breathed, stretching out a hand towards him. 'Dion, don't go. Please ...'

He halted, but he did not turn to look at her, and with a sound of impatience she scrambled on to her knees and reached for his ankle. 'Dion,' she repeated huskily, 'do you remember how we used to take baths together? Do you remember how we used to share—everything?'

'*Hristo*, Martha, do you want me to despise myself even more than I do already?' he groaned, looking down at her now, but when she silently shook her head, he was unable to resist the alluring temptation of her. 'This is madness!' he protested, but his fingers were already unloosening the cord of his bathrobe, and dropping it carelessly on to the tiles, he stepped down into the water.

Martha's mouth was warm and moist from the steamy atmosphere, her body slippery with soap, but infinitely sensuous, coiling against him, with all the unconscious sexuality of her nature. Dion would not have been human if he had not responded to it, and with an urgency born of his own needs he drew her down with him into the scented depths.

'Love me,' she whispered against his lips, the intimacy of their embrace heightening her already stimulated senses, inspiring a mindless abandon in which constraint had no part. She wanted him, she wanted to please him, and she wanted the closeness that only total possession could give.

'I want to,' he muttered in return, his half closed eyes devouring her. 'I do not think you could stop me now ...'

'Not here,' she objected, half in panic, when his mouth

parted hers once again, but he only held her closer.

'Why not?' he countered, with devastating frankness, and she could think of no significant reason to deny him.

It was like drowning, she thought imaginatively, only that awful fate offered nothing to compare with the sensations Dion was inspiring. Yet the release of all conscious control on one's actions was like the drifting, dreaming, yielding, of a leaf on the tide, and there was only the warmth and the water and Dion, and sensuous, sensual feeling ...

Afterwards, he lifted her out of the water and carried her into their bedroom, laying her on the bed and making love to her all over again. When she protested about the dampness of the sheets, he only smiled and said that they only needed half the bed to sleep in anyway, and she was too satiated and drowsy with emotion to care about anything but that he should remain with her. She had never felt such ecstasy, such soaring rapture, and she responded without volition, pleasing him as he was pleasing her, until exhaustion drove them to seek a shared oblivion ...

CHAPTER TEN

MARTHA awakened the next morning with a feeling of relief so intense, she felt almost weak with reaction. Nothing could ever be the same again, not after last night, and however Dion had behaved in the past, she believed he loved her now, and that was the most important thing of all. His lovemaking had been so much more than just a simple gratification of the senses. It had been a declaration of their need for one another. A union of minds as well as bodies, as satisfying as it had been beautiful.

Turning over, she was slightly disconcerted to find the bed beside her empty, and a puzzled little frown furrowed the wide smoothness of her forehead. A probing hand produced the knowledge that the sheet beside her was still faintly warm, a sure indication that it had not been long since Dion's departure.

Rolling over, she focussed on the clock standing on the table beside the bed, experiencing a sense of astonishment when she discovered it was already after eleven. After *eleven*! she echoed silently, blinking in amazement. No wonder she was alone!

Pushing one slender leg out of bed, she was delightfully shocked to discover her own nakedness, and she stood for a few moments before the vanity mirror, giving in to a little vanity of her own. Dion's lovemaking had left more than merely physical marks upon her, and the languorous darkness of her eyes held a secret all their own. Her tongue appeared in teasing provocation, and then, with a half smile of satisfaction, she sought the satin wrapper she had discarded before the previous evening's party.

She was brushing the tangled disorder of her hair when there was a tentative tap at the bedroom door, and her heart leapt alarmingly at the prospect of seeing her husband again. But it was only Irene, her maid, who entered the apartment, her smile appearing shyly when she discovered Martha was awake.

'Kirios Dionysus asked me not to disturb you this morning, madame,' she murmured, in half apology for her absence, but Martha made an expansive gesture, dismissing her excuses.

'That's all right, Irene,' she assured her, in her own language. 'But I'd love some coffee, if there's some available, and do you know where Kirios Dionysus is?'

'I think he went out, madame. With Kirios Myconos,' replied Irene doubtfully. 'I will get the coffee. Five minutes, madame.'

After she had gone, Martha's spirits sank a little. So Dion had gone out. Why should it matter to her? They were supposedly leaving for Mycos this afternoon. She would have his undivided attention soon enough, and to-night ...

Refusing to allow such disturbing thoughts to disrupt her composure, Martha went into the bathroom to wash, and clean her teeth. Its cream and gold luxury brought back memories of their closeness the night before, and she brushed her teeth more vigorously than she might have done, trying to divert the inclination of her thoughts.

She had dressed, in slim-fitting cotton pants and a matching smock of apricot lace, when Irene returned with her tray, and the Greek girl's eyes widened in admiration as she took in the charming picture Martha presented.

'You look so young to have already a five-year-old daughter,' she exclaimed, half enviously, and Martha felt a twinge of remorse at the awareness of how little thought she had given to her daughter since Dion had taken her in his arms.

'Thank you,' she said now, pouring herself a cup of the steaming black liquid and sipping it appreciatively. 'Hmm, this is delicious. Will you thank Kiria Marcos for me?'

'I made it myself,' confessed Irene shyly, and Martha felt a surge of affection towards her. 'Kiria Myconos is asking to see you, and I knew you would not wish to keep her waiting.'

'Kiria Myconos?' Martha felt a faint touch of disquiet. 'Ariadne? She wants to see me? Oh, lord! Why? Do you know?'

Irene bent her head. 'I am sorry, I only know that Kiria Myconos asks you to speak with her as soon as you are dressed, madame. She is waiting for you in the library.'

Martha sighed, but she nodded understandingly at Irene, thanking her for the coffee and for delivering the message. 'I expect she wants to ask why Dion and I left the party so early last night,' she murmured, half to herself, though she doubted Ariadne would be as unsubtle as that. 'Will you tell Kirios Dionysus where I am, if he comes back in the meantime,' she added, and Irene agreed that she would.

Her mother-in-law surveyed her appearance without enthusiasm when Martha announced herself in the doorway to the library. Ariadne did not approve of trousers on women and never wore them herself, and her other daughters-in-law were too plump to want to oppose her in this way.

'So,' she said, speaking in English for a change, 'you have chosen to awaken at last. After the early night you had, I would have expected you to be—how do you say it?—up with the birds this morning.'

'Lark,' said Martha automatically. 'Up with the lark,' she added, by way of an explanation, though her lips twitched a little in amused recollection. If Ariadne only knew, she thought humorously, how little sleep she had actually had! 'I'm sorry, I didn't know you were waiting to speak to me.'

'No. No, I do not suppose you did,' agreed Ariadne
dryly, indicating a leather banquette beneath the windows.
'Will you sit down? There are things which I think you and
I must discuss.'

Martha remembered another occasion when one of
Dion's parents had offered her a seat and politely declined.
Whatever Ariadne had to say, she would hear standing up,
and her mother-in-law made a dismissing gesture with her
hands as she sought the comfort of a tapestry-covered
sofa.

'Very well,' she said, arranging the folds of her morning
gown around her. 'As you may have guessed, it is about
my son that I wish to speak, and I should like you to tell
me exactly what the situation is between you two.'

'The situation?' Martha played for time, moving her
shoulders in an unknowingly sensuous gesture. 'But you
know the situation, madame.'

'Do I?' Ariadne shrugged. 'When you persistently call
me madame, and not Mama, as you know I would wish?'

'I'm sorry.'

'No matter.' Ariadne shook her head. 'I am persuaded
that will come in time. After Dionysus' behaviour last
evening, it is no longer in any doubt that he intends we
should accept you.' She paused, and Martha shifted a little
uncomfortably under her gaze. 'You know to what I am
referring, of course.'

Martha nodded. 'Miss Kuriakin.'

'Miss Kuriakin, as you say.' The older woman shook her
head. 'My son is not normally so discourteous. However,
that is not what I wish to discuss with you.'

'No, mad—Mama.'

Ariadne acknowledged this attempt to placate her with a
faint smile, and then said, more seriously: 'It is my wish
that Dionysus should have no more unhappiness in his life.'

'That is my wish, too,' agreed Martha eagerly, and her
mother-in-law frowned.

'Yet you cannot deny that you have made my son's life a torment for him in the past,' she asserted. 'I would not want that to happen again.'

'It won't,' declared Martha, without hesitation. 'I love Dion—Mama. I always have. I guess I always will.'

'But can you deny he had virtually to—to blackmail you to persuade you to come out to the islands?'

Martha sighed. 'He told you?'

'No.' Ariadne's nostrils flared. 'No, he told me nothing—he seldom does. Alex told me. Alex was concerned about him. We all were. And these past few days have been no reassurance to us. Oh, you have been together, I cannot deny that. You have shared the same suite of rooms. Yet I am told Dionysus occupies a bed in his dressing room, and you are only polite to one another when you join the family for meals.'

Martha bent her head, embarrassment bringing a faint colour to her cheeks. 'We—I—that is, it—it hasn't been easy for us—Mama. We needed—time.'

'Needed?'

'Yes.' Martha lifted her head then. 'I don't think Dion will be sleeping in his dressing room any longer.'

'I see.' Ariadne surveyed her closely, and Martha had great difficulty in sustaining that regard. 'So—I am relieved. But that still leaves one matter to be resolved: that of your sister. I understand she has accompanied you to Mycos.'

'That's right.' Martha wondered how Sarah came into this. 'You sound as if you don't—approve.'

Ariadne snorted. 'Approve! Martha, do not pretend you do not understand my feelings. That woman has been the bane of Dionysus's life, of all our lives. When my sons suffer, I suffer, too.'

Martha linked her trembling fingers together. 'Sarah was not to blame for our break-up, Mama,' she insisted. 'Have you never asked yourself how you would have acted, faced

with a husband who believed the child you had borne hir
was some other man's?'

'And why did he believe it?' retorted her mother-in-la
sharply. 'Have you never asked yourself that?'

Martha's brows were drawing together in growing dis
belief, when the door behind her opened and someone cam
in. She half turned reluctantly, afraid if it was her husban
of what she might see in his face, then felt her knees buck
ling when she met Dion's dark anxious eyes. She had n
need to ask what he was thinking: it was there in his fac
for her to see. And uncaring of Ariadne's disapprova
Martha covered the space between them in eager anticipa
tion.

Dion's hands at her waist prevented a more ardent em
brace, but the kiss that he bestowed in the hollow behin
her ear was made all the more intimate by the probin
caress of his tongue. He did it deliberately, she knew, look
ing up into his smouldering eyes, and his muffled: 'Do no
look at me like that!' was for her ears alone.

Ariadne, who had watched this exchange with surprisin
sympathy, now continued her conversation. Addressing he
remarks to Dion, instead of Martha, she enlarged upon he
theme, bringing a look of intense irritation to his lean dar
features.

'I gather you have not spoken to Martha about he
sister,' she exclaimed incredulously, getting up from th
sofa. 'You are a fool, Dionysus. After all these waste
years——'

'We will not discuss this again, Mama!' he interrupte
her brusquely, and Martha was chilled by the way he pu
her aside. 'The past is dead and gone. We will not resur
rect it.'

'But, Dion——'

'No, Mama.' His eyes were glacial now. 'I do not wis
you to mention it ever again. And now, if you will excus

us, there are matters to attend to before our departure this afternoon.'

His mother had no choice but to dismiss them, and Martha preceded him up the stairs in a state of some anxiety. What did it all mean? What was Sarah supposed to have done? Was it just an extension of Dion's dislike of her sister, or had there been some other reason for the things Ariadne had said?

In their room, she waited until the door was closed, and then she said: 'I think you ought to tell me what all that was about. I know what you said to your mother, but don't I have a right to know?'

Dion sighed. 'There is nothing to know, Martha,' he declared quietly. 'My—er—my family is very loyal. They only want us to be happy.'

Martha still looked troubled. 'And are we?' she ventured, tentatively. 'Are we happy, Dion?'

His eyes darkened. 'You regret what happened last night?'

'Regret it?' Martha sought an answer in the ceiling. 'No, of course *I* don't regret it.'

'You think I do?' he exclaimed incredulously.

She shook her head. 'I don't know. I don't know what you think.'

Dion's oath of protest died in the curtain of her hair as he jerked her urgently towards him, pressing her close against the muscular hardness of his body. 'If you do not know how I feel about you now, you never will,' he muttered incoherently. '*Theos*, Martha, you are my soul, my love, my life ...'

She trembled as his mouth sought hers, but his passion demanded a response, and her arms wound themselves about his neck, without thought of denial. It was only when he lifted his lips that the doubting words escaped her, and his anguish was evident in the deeply etched lines beside his mouth.

'And—and Josy?' she whispered, needing his reassurance, and he expelled his breath on a heavy sigh as he pushed her away from him.

'So,' he said. 'She still comes between us.'

'Between us?' Martha did not understand. 'Dion, I only want to know——'

'—how I could deny her?' he finished wearily, but she shook her head.

'No. No, not that.' And at his frowning uncertainty: 'Dion, is it only Josy that's bringing us back together? Is it for her sake you're willing to forget the past?'

'For *her* sake?' He stared at her.

'Yes, for her sake. And your own. Because she's your daughter. Because ...' She found it almost impossible to go on. 'Because if it is, I would have to let—to let her go.'

'To let her go?' His incredulity was riveting. 'Forgive me if I seem a little dense, but what are you saying?'

Martha shifted restlessly from one foot to the other. 'Oh, you know what I mean,' she protested. 'Dion, do you really love me? I know you want me, you can't deny that, but is this desire to take me back not just because you want to claim your daughter?'

He swore in Greek, but she understood him, and with a gesture of impatience he hauled her round to face him. 'Is that what you think?' he groaned. 'Is that really what you think? After everything we have been to one another?'

'It's not what I want to think,' she confessed huskily, gazing up at him. 'But I have to know. I—I couldn't bear it if we—if we separated again.'

'You could not bear it,' he muttered, half in irony. 'Oh, my love, I think it would kill me!'

'Dion——'

His mouth silenced whatever else she had planned to say, and the minutes stretched as he continued to hold her. But at last he dragged his mouth from hers, straightening her smock and saying rather thickly: 'Do you know that was what I had to ask you? Have you forgiven me? Are you really prepared to take me as I am, flawed and selfish?'

Martha cupped his face in her hands. 'I have to,' she said simply and honestly. 'I love you—I always have. I only persuaded myself I didn't to protect my own sanity.'

Dion's thumbs explored the hollows of her ears. 'You know I did not intend this to happen. Not yet, at any rate,' he conceded, at the widening indignation in her eyes. 'You have not really had the time to get to know me again—my faults, my possessiveness. You used to say I treated you like a possession. Can you honestly believe you can live with that again?'

'I can't live without it,' Martha whispered huskily. 'But I won't promise that we won't argue sometimes.'

'I would not have it any other way,' he told her gently, bending his lips to her shoulder.

'Are you really going to take me to New York?' Martha asked, remembering what he had said the night before with real enthusiasm now, and he nodded rather humorously.

'That is one thing that has to change,' he affirmed, his hands probing beneath her smock once more, and spreading against the curve of her spine. 'It has been the way of my family to leave their women behind, but I intend to alter all that. I want you with me. And Josy, too, sometimes. That is why I have employed Miss Powell. But mostly, I do not intend that you should have to seek entertainment with anyone other than your husband, no?'

Martha smiled. 'I trust you, you know.'

Dion shook his head. 'I know. And I did not trust you.'

'I didn't mean that.'

'No, but I did,' he averred huskily. 'Can you ever forget what I said?'

Martha pressed her lips together for a moment. Then she said quietly: 'Can you forgive me for taking her away? For letting you go on thinking what you did——'

'I should never have suspected you!' he broke in impatiently, but she only shook her head.

'We're all human,' she pointed out gently. 'We all have our faults. We are all selfish sometimes, and we all need reassurance.'

Dion touched her mouth with his tongue. 'Reassure me now,' he murmured, his hands arching her body sensuously, and Martha could think of nothing she would like more.

It was late afternoon when the helicopter set them down near the harbour on Mycos. Alex himself had come to meet them, and another small body came hurtling at them as they detached themselves from the cabin.

'Mummy! Mummy! Uncle Dion!' Josy squealed excitedly, and Martha exchanged a look of understanding with her husband as she bent to hug their daughter.

'Have you been good, darling?' Martha asked her, after Josy had hugged Dion, too, and was walking happily between them, back to where Alex was waiting with the station wagon. 'You're getting really brown. I expect you've spent all your time in the pool, haven't you?'

'She would like to,' put in Alex dryly, hesitating only a moment before kissing Martha on both cheeks. 'Welcome home, sister. I gather it has been a good trip.'

Martha coloured appealingly, but Dion relieved her embarrassment. 'Very good,' he agreed, his mouth humorous as he watched the younger man. 'And do you not just envy me that knowledge, little brother?'

On the journey up to the house, Alex asked less personal questions—how were their parents, had the Stavros deal gone through, when was Dion leaving for the United States —and Josy took the opportunity to tell her mother all that had happened since she went away.

'Auntie Sarah doesn't like Jill,' she confided, shattering Martha's newly-found contentment at a stroke. 'She called her a—a fortune-hunter, and Jill said she was an—an old hag? Isn't that right, Uncle Alex?'

Now it was Alex's turn to look embarrassed. 'You ought not to repeat such things, Josy,' he reproved, concentrating on his driving, but after a quick glance at his wife's face Dion took up the theme.

'I gather you are involved,' he remarked shrewdly, as his brother's neck turned red. 'What have you been doing? Turning the girl's head?'

'No!' Alex hunched his shoulders over the wheel. 'I may have showed her some attention. Why not? She is a pretty girl. But nothing to get so—so choked up about. Sarah is jealous, that is all. You know that. You should do —you of all people!'

Dion ignored this, although once again Martha was obliged to accept that so far as the Myconos family was concerned, Sarah was *persona non grata.* 'So,' he said. 'There was a row, was there? And what happened after this confrontation?'

'Well ...' Alex hesitated, 'Scott was there, too, as it happened, and he managed to smooth things over.' He glanced round at Martha, sitting with Josy in the back. 'He managed to—make light of the situation, and since then he has taken Sarah out with him on his—explorations.'

'Taken Sarah?' Martha echoed disbelievingly. 'But— how can he?'

'They go in the buggy,' declared Josy, not to be out-done.

'The jeep,' declared Alex flatly. 'It is a four-wheel-drive vehicle, and can cover most terrain.'

'I see.' Dion moved his shoulders dismissively. 'And— Miss Powell? Jill? How did she react to this—argument?'

'Oh, Jill laughed about it afterwards,' Josy volunteered, forestalling him again. 'It was funny really. Everyone with red faces!'

'Since when do you call Miss Powell Jill?' enquired

Martha, more sharply than she might have done, still on edge after these revelations, and Josy pulled a face.

'Since always,' she retorted, rather impudently. '*Miss Powell* is old-fashioned—she said so.'

Martha sighed, and Dion turned to stretch out his hand towards her. 'Do not worry,' he adjured, when she put her hand into his, and felt its reassuring strength. 'I will sort everything out, I promise.'

Josy looked surprised at this unexpected display of affection, and her brows descended mutinously. 'Hold my hand, Mummy,' she said, pulling Martha's away from her father's. 'I can look after you, can't I?'

Dion's expression did not change as he looked at his daughter. 'You and I are both going to look after Mummy from now on,' he told her, gently but insistently. 'I married your mother a long time ago, Josy, and now I am going to take care of her.'

Martha had never expected he would tell her like that. If she had thought about it at all, it was in terms of him mentioning it at some distant date, when Josy was older and wiser, and more capable of assimilating it.

But now she realised he was right. The younger Josy was, the less she had to understand, and like all adults, she had judged the situation from an adult's point of view, seeing only the difficulties involved and not the simplicity of it. To Josy, being married was something entirely different from what it meant to her, and the closeness of their relationship, the fact that they would sleep together from now on, meant simply that in a child's mind.

Even so, Josy was old enough to appreciate a little of what this might mean to her in terms of her exclusive rights to her mother's attention, and turning to Martha now, she said, half tearfully, half crossly: 'I didn't want you to get married! I don't want to share you with Uncle Dion! I want you all to myself!'

Martha sighed, tempted to comfort her, but aware of the

importance of the occasion. 'Darling, I didn't *just* get married, I've been married all along. We—we just didn't live together for a while, that's all. But that's over now. We're all together again. And you have a daddy and a mummy now.'

Josy's lips quivered. 'Uncle Dion's not my daddy! He said he was a *friend* of my daddy's.'

'I'm sorry, I could not tell you before,' Dion confessed gently. 'You would not have believed me.'

Josy sniffed, not quite knowing how to take this. 'Does that mean we're always going to live here?'

'Here—or in Athens,' agreed Dion, nodding. 'And soon you will meet all your other aunts and uncles and cousins, and even your grandmama and grandpapa in time.'

Josy perked up. 'I have cousins?' she questioned disbelievingly. 'Real cousins?'

'Lots of them,' agreed Martha dryly.

'But no brothers or sisters,' Josy mused thoughtfully, and Dion said dryly: 'Not yet.'

Josy gasped. 'Might I have?' she exclaimed, staring at her mother now, wide-eyed. 'Might you have a baby? A real baby?'

'Soon, I hope,' agreed Martha, meeting Dion's eyes above their daughter's head, knowing that that particular obstacle would never trouble them again, and Josy absorbed this new information with obviously more enthusiasm.

As he helped her out of the car, however, Dion held Martha to him for a moment. 'You did not mind, did you?' he probed, his eyes dark and liquid soft as they held hers. 'My telling Josy, I mean.'

'Why should I?' she countered, reaching up to kiss him, and he had to steel himself not to return her salute more thoroughly.

'I did not want to give Sarah that weapon over us,' he confessed huskily. 'Now Josy knows, no one can hurt her.'

The other members of the household were on the patio, waiting to greet them, although Martha suspected it was Roger's doing that Sarah was there at all. He was sitting between her and Jill Powell, and it was obvious from his expression that he was glad of their arrival to provide a diversion.

'Hey!' he exclaimed, after Martha had bent to kiss her sister's rigid cheek. 'You look—different. More relaxed, somehow. Now who would have thought that you'd relax in a city like Athens, when you haven't relaxed at all while you've been here!'

'Perhaps it was the freedom from responsibilities that did it,' suggested Jill, smiling her welcome. 'You do look well, Madame Myconos. Did you have a good trip?'

'Marvellous!' Martha assured her warmly, trying to ignore Sarah's inimical stare, and was glad that Jill excused herself to order some tea, when Josy danced on to the patio chanting: 'I've got a daddy and a mummy!' with apparent disregard for her earlier reservations.

'I gather you've told her,' Sarah remarked, making her first comment since their return. 'Don't you think that was rather presumptuous in the circumstances?'

'What circumstances?' Martha glanced awkwardly towards Dion, and he came to rest his arm possessively across her shoulders.

'Yes. What circumstances, Sarah?' he asked bleakly, showing her none of the consideration he had shown when he spoke to Jill Powell. 'Exactly what would you have had Martha do? Remain virtually a widow, for the rest of her life? Continually paying for the mistake of loving me?'

'Oh, Dion, please ...' Martha didn't think she could bear to witness any more unpleasantness, but Sarah was determined to have her way.

'You admit it was a mistake, then, Dion,' she countered, maliciously. 'Is that why you were so eager to get rid of her that you even denied your own child?'

'Sarah, I warn you——'

Dion's mouth was hard and angry, and Alex moved rather uncomfortably in the background. But it was Roger who intervened at this point, taking the onus upon himself as he said quietly:

'I think I ought to tell you that I've persuaded Sarah to marry me, Martha. Or at least, I've persuaded her to consider the idea. You three don't need anyone else to complete your happiness, I can see that, while I—I do need Sarah's caustic tongue to keep me in order.'

'Such a romantic proposal,' sneered Sarah coldly. 'I told Roger I had no intention of marrying anyone so long as you needed me, Martha. But obviously you felt no such commitment.'

'Sarah, I love Dion——' Martha felt Josy beside her, and put her hand on the little girl's shoulder in reassurance. 'Isn't it better that we're a family again, than living a life apart?'

'If you can bear to live with a man who was fool enough to abandon you, then I suppose the answer's yes!' declared Sarah contemptuously, and with a groan of compulsion, Roger erupted angrily.

'For God's sake, Sarah!' he swore furiously, his angular face flushed and rueful. 'I didn't want to say this, but I'm going to have to. Dion would never have accused Martha of having a lover without your intervention!'

There was silence after his accusation, a silence that was only broken by Josy's whispered pleas as to what was the matter, and Alex moved quickly, taking the little girl's hand and suggesting that if she put on her bathing suit, he would teach her a new game in the pool.

Josy hesitated, but was diverted, and Martha let her go with a sick feeling of confusion. She didn't understand any of this, and she wished someone would explain.

Roger raked back his hair now with unsteady fingers, gazing at Dion entreatingly, appealing for his understanding. Then, when the other man still said nothing, he continued awkwardly: 'Martha has to be told, Dion. It's the only way.'

'Told? Told what?' Martha pleaded now, turning to her husband with bewildered eyes. 'This has to do with what your mother said earlier, hasn't it? Oh, Dion, tell me, tell me! Don't make Roger do it for you.'

'I'll tell you,' said Sarah chokingly, her hands clenched on the arms of her chair. 'If you want to know, I'll tell you, although Dion swore me to silence when he came to the house two months ago.'

Martha shook her head. 'Dion swore you to silence?' she echoed, and her husband sighed.

'I saw no reason why you should be hurt any more than you had been,' he declared heavily. 'But if Sarah wants to tell you, I cannot stop her.'

'So noble!' snapped Sarah spitefully, but Roger's hand upon her shoulder prevented any harsher outburst. 'Anyway, you may as well know—I never wanted you to marry him,' she declared offhandedly. 'But then you did know that, didn't you?'

'You didn't aprove,' agreed Martha, frowning. 'But what has that to do with this?'

Sarah shrugged, and then, as if deciding only honesty would suffice, she said: 'I hated you, Martha. I hated you for tricking me and sucking up to Dion whenever my back was turned——'

'It wasn't like that,' protested Martha in horror, but her sister was already going on.

'—and I hated you most of all when you got him to marry you by the oldest method in the book!'

'That's not true!'

Martha was sickened, but she felt Dion's hand squeeze her shoulder insistently, and realised it was just the outpourings of her sister's jealous mind ... as *he* had always said.

'Well, you married him,' said Sarah grimly, 'and for a while I thought there was nothing I could do. But then,' she paused, 'Dion became involved with the company, and you began to get bored——'

'Not bored!'

'Restless, then. Jealous of the time he spent away from you. Eager to do something—anything—to make him notice you again.' She shrugged. 'It was easy. I encouraged you to come to London. Roger was always around. It was simple to convince Dion that you came to see him.'

'But how could you convince Dion of a thing like that?' asked Martha blankly, unable to comprehend, and with an oath her husband supplied the answer.

'She wrote me,' he declared, his fingers biting into her shoulder. 'Look, need we go on? I think the situation has been satisfactorily explained. I was a fool—I think we are all agreed on that. But I can assure you, I have learnt my lesson well.'

Martha licked her lips. 'But what did—she say in her letters?' she protested faintly. 'Dion, Roger was her friend, not mine.'

'I know that now,' Dion whispered wearily. 'My darling, we have more to thank Roger for than you know.' He paused. 'When he discovered that Sarah had written to me, he devised this plan to get you to contact me. He guessed that my father would show me your letter, and he was right.'

'But how did you find out Sarah had written to Dion?' exclaimed Martha helplessly. 'Surely she didn't tell you?'

Roger shook his head. 'You know when we went to the Scillies last summer?' he said. 'I helped Sarah to unpack on our return. I found some papers at the bottom of her wardrobe——'

'—and he looked at them!' declared Sarah resentfully.

'I thought they were mine,' Roger protested steadily. 'Martha had been collating my notes for me. I thought they must have got mixed up with Sarah's belongings by mistake.'

'Oh, Sarah!' Martha could hardly bear to look at her. 'I could have found them myself at any time!'

'I like to think she hoped you would,' said Roger, sighing. 'Anyway, you know now, and that's the main thing.'

'Yes.' Martha looked entreatingly at her husband. 'Oh, Dion, I don't know what to say to you.'

'Do not say anything,' he advised her gently. 'Like you said, we all make mistakes.'

'But you should have told me! When you found out, you should have told me.'

'I did not care to be the one to tell you such things,' he said heavily. 'Sarah and I—well, we were never destined to be friends. How could I destroy your trust in her? I thought—I hoped it would not be necessary.'

'Don't give me any handouts, Dion,' snapped Sarah malevolently. 'I don't need anything from you.'

'Sarah!' Roger's tone was a warning. Then he looked at Dion. 'We're leaving, actually. We've just been waiting for you two to come back to tell you. Sarah doesn't get along with Jill, and I guess I've done all the exploring I need on Mycos. We're moving on to Santorini. I'm hoping to meet up with the chaps who are working at Akrotiri. But thanks anyway, for letting me have this time.'

'Thank *you*,' said Dion fervently, his grim features breaking into a faint smile. 'I know I said I did not want this to happen, but perhaps it is better this way.'

'Thanks.' Roger appreciated the gesture. 'I'm sure we'll all get over it in time.'

'I won't,' declared Sarah vehemently, and Martha doubted she could either.

Alone in their room later, Martha found it impossible to justify Sarah's behaviour towards her husband. He had done nothing to warrant such hatred in her sister, and she wished there was some way she could make up to him for all that he had suffered.

'I can't understand why I never suspected anything,' she fretted now, seated before the vanity unit, unhappily regarding her reflection in the mirror. 'In all those years I never dreamt she might have been involved.'

'Why would you?' Dion countered gently, coming to stand behind her. 'So far as you were concerned, Sarah was on your side. She had agreed with you, sympathised with you, done everything to make you believe she had only your well-being at heart. Why should you suspect her?'

Martha shook her head. 'I should have remembered how she acted when I told her we were getting married. But I thought she had got over that.' Then she frowned. 'Tell me about the letters. How could you believe what she wrote, knowing how she felt about you?'

Dion sighed, drawing her back against his thighs. 'I suppose she played on our weakness for one another,' he said at last. 'She was clever, I see that now.'

'But when did she contact you? When did you begin to suspect me?'

Dion hesitated. 'Well, if you insist on hearing it all ...' He frowned. 'I suppose the first time she wrote to me was about a year before our separation——'

'A year!' Martha was horrified, and Dion shook his head.

'Are you sure you want to hear this?' he demanded huskily. 'It is all over now.'

'No.' Martha held up her head. 'I want to know—I *have* to know. Go on, please. I'm sorry I interrupted you.'

Dion's mouth compressed, but after a moment he continued: 'It was just after a visit you had made to London. She wrote that—oh, that you had been seeing Scott while you were in London, and that naturally she was upset. They were thinking of getting engaged, she explained, and —well, you were trying to split them up.'

'*No!*'

Martha's lips parted in dismay, and Dion's hands slid possessively over her shoulders, 'Would you rather I did not go on?' he exclaimed. 'Martha, there is no point in torturing yourself this way.'

'If only you'd told me!' she protested tremulously, and he nodded his head slowly, in acknowledgement of his own doubts in not doing so. 'So—what happened then?'

'*Kala*,' Dion made an impatient gesture, 'that was when I tried to stop you from visiting London so frequently.'

'And I thought you were jealous,' murmured Martha wonderingly, and his mouth assumed a mocking curve.

'Oh, I was,' he assured her, his hands caressing. 'Very jealous. Increasingly so, when you persistently ignored my requests.'

Martha was appalled. 'Sarah knows me. She knows me so well. She knew if you tried to stop me from doing something I would rebel against it.'

Dion shrugged. 'Well, I need not elaborate. There was more of the same, and over a period of time I could not help but believe what was happening, particularly when you seemed so eager to visit your sister.'

'Sarah encouraged me. She said she was lonely. She said that since I'd got married, she had no one.'

'She had Scott,' declared Dion heavily. 'Only I was too blind to see it.'

'So—so when Josy was born with—with red hair——'

Dion nodded. 'Disaster!'

'But—but Sarah's hair is auburn!'

'I know.' Dion sighed again. 'I guess I was not thinking with my brain, only with my emotions.'

'And Sarah told you the child was Roger's?'

'Oh, no, she was too clever for that. But she had hinted in one of her letters how embarrassing it would be for you if the child had red hair.'

'Oh, God!'

Martha buried her face in her hands, and felt his hands moving on her neck. 'So you see why Sarah and I have no love for one another,' he said gently. 'She knew once I had seen Josy again there was no way she could continue deceiving me, on that score at least.'

'And—and the rest? My relationship with—with Roger?'

'Learning that Josy was mine put an entirely new light on the situation. And once I had met—Roger, I guessed where his sympathies lay.'

'Oh, Dion!'

'It is strange how these things happen, is it not?' he mused. 'Maybe if Sarah had not had the accident, you would not have moved into Roger's house, no?'

'Possibly not, although we needed more space, for—for the baby.'

'*Our* baby,' agreed Dion, with some satisfaction.

'Our daughter,' murmured Martha huskily. 'Darling, I don't know how to make it up to you.'

'It is enough that you were prepared to accept me without knowing the whole truth of the situation,' he declared roughly. 'But now all is clear between us. We can start again.'

Six months later, Dion came to find Martha as she was dressing for dinner one evening, a telegram in his hand.

'This has just arrived,' he said, handing it to her, and she turned her back for him to fasten her zipper while she read the telegram's contents.

The message was from Roger, short and simple—he and Sarah had been married that morning, at the register office in Wimbledon, with only a couple of his colleagues and their wives as witnesses.

Dion turned her to face him as she looked up from the paper, the arch of his brows indicating the enquiry in her eyes.

'You are not sorry, are you?' he asked, lifting her chin with his finger, and she caught his fingers with hers, and carried them to her lips.

'No,' she said firmly. 'It was much too soon. And Roger will understand that if Sarah doesn't.'

'I would have gone with you,' Dion told her quietly. 'If you had really wished to attend——'

'I didn't,' said Martha, holding his palm against her cheek. 'Maybe when they have their first baby, then it will be different.'

'Roger says in his letter that the therapy is working,' remarked Dion gently, his fingers sliding round her nape. 'Who knows, one day she may walk again and confound us all. Anyway, I hope she is happy.'

'You're very generous,' said Martha with a sigh the agony of the past still too close to dismiss, but Dion only shook his head.

'Why should I not be?' he countered, drawing her to him. 'With the most beautiful wife in Athens, and a daughter who fills her grandparents with delight.' His hand probed the swelling roundness of her stomach beneath the generously proportioned gown. 'Not to mention the reason why I have delegated most of my travelling to Alex until the spring, when you can join me again.'

Martha nestled against him, loving the feel of his hands on her body. 'Josy is so excited. Do you think she'll really adjust to the baby without feeling put out?'

'The way my mother dotes on her, you would think she had no other grandchildren,' asserted Dion dryly, his lips seeking the curve of her cheek. 'Now, do we go down for dinner, or do I unzip this most beautiful gown once again? I warn you, if you continue to move against me as you are doing, you may have no choice in the matter.'

Martha's low laughter was warm and intimate. 'Oh Dion, I'm so happy,' she whispered, and he took a few moments to show his appreciation.

Titles available this month in the Mills & Boon ROMANCE Series

THE KURRANULLA ROUND *by Dorothy Cork*
Matty's uncle wanted to see her married to Dirk Reasoner,
but Matty knew something her uncle didn't — and that was
why Dirk would never trust and respect her, let alone love
her . . .

ACROSS THE GREAT DIVIDE *by Kerry Allyne*
It was Jerome whom Nicole loved — so why was it the annoying Lang Jamieson who occupied so much of her thoughts?

FLAME OF DIABLO *by Sara Craven*
Vitas de Mendoza agreed to help Rachel find her brother —
but at a price. Would she find the price too high? Or would
she pay — far too willingly?

BLUE LOTUS *by Margaret Way*
Susan was rescued from the rain forest of Queensland by
Devin Chandler and taken to recover at his cattle station — a
private kingdom where the king made his own laws . . .

FRUSTRATION *by Charlotte Lamb*
Considering the tumultuous circumstances of their first
meeting, it was hardly surprising that Jake Lang should
despise and dislike Natalie Buchan . . .

A DANGEROUS MAN *by Mary Wibberley*
When Tania met Bryden Kane she realised that he was a
dangerous man to know — certainly she could sense the
danger to her own heart.

APOLLO'S SEED *by Anne Mather*
Martha had been virtually forced to return to Greece and her
husband Dion. But it was clear that his only reason for wanting
her was to get their child back.

A MAN TO WATCH *by Jane Donnelly*
To Harriet, Jotham Gaul was nothing but an irritating boor
who told her she had nothing but her looks — but why should
she care about his opinion?

A CERTAIN SMILE *by Marjorie Lewty*
When Amanda discovered her father, she found herself
whisked into a world of wealth, of tycoons, of sophistication
— and a world that also contained Blair Craddock . . .

STORMY AFFAIR *by Margaret Mayo*
Who did Hamed Ben Slouma think he was, spoiling Amber's
peaceful holiday in Tunisia by whisking her off to his house
and announcing that he was going to marry her?

Mills & Boon Romances
— all that's pleasurable in Romantic Reading!

Available November 1979

The Mills & Boon Rose is the Rose of Romance

Look for the Rose of Romance this Christmas

Four titles by favourite authors in a specially-produced gift pack.

THAT BOSTON MAN *by Janet Dailey*

MY SISTER'S KEEPER *by Rachel Lindsay*

ENEMY FROM THE PAST *by Lilian Peake*

DARK DOMINION *by Charlotte Lamb*

UNITED KINGDOM £2.20 net
REP. OF IRELAND £2.40

First time in paperback. Published 12th October.
You can obtain this gift pack from your local paperback retailer.

Also available this month
Four titles in our Mills & Boon
Classics Series
*Specially chosen reissues of the best in
Romantic Fiction*

November 's Titles are:

WIFE FOR A PENNY
by Anne Hampson

If Liz didn't marry Nigel Shapani two family fortunes would
be lost, under the terms of an eccentric will. So she married
him, and he took her off to his home in Greece. But it was to
be a business arrangement only. She would never let herself
fall in love with him — to a Greek love, in a woman, meant
subservience, and Liz would never stand for that. But was Liz
really as strong-minded as she thought she was?

THE NIGHT OF THE HURRICANE
by Andrea Blake

Julie's idyllic life on a lonely Caribbean island ended when
her father remarried and her stepmother tried to persuade
him to sell the place. Even after her marriage to Simon Tiernan,
Julie felt her stepmother's malicious influence.

MASK OF SCARS
by Anne Mather

Christina's brother was running a hotel in the Algarve, in
southern Portugal, so when her long vacation came along, it
struck her as a good idea to go and spend it with him. At any
rate, it seemed a good idea until she realised just how unwelcome she was! Nevertheless, she soon began to wonder if she
had done the right thing when she took the job offered her
by the local lord of the manor . . .

A MAN OF AFFAIRS
(The Widening Stream)
by Rachel Lindsay

When Melanie Powell became engaged to an American, she
invited her friend Loris Cameron to accompany her on a visit
to his family home in California, and on the way Loris too
fell in love — with Brett Halliday. But both girls were to have
a long way to travel before they reached the end of their
journey to happiness.

Mills & Boon Classics
— all that's great in Romantic Reading!

BUY THEM TODAY

The Mills & Boon Rose is the Rose of Romance

Look for the Mills & Boon Rose next month

TEMPLE OF THE DAWN *by Anne Hampson*
Lexa lost her heart to Paul Mansell — but his heart belonged,
as it always would, to his beautiful dead wife Sally ...

MY DARLING SPITFIRE *by Rosemary Carter*
The only way Siane could join her fiancé on a remote game
reserve was to go in the company of the *maddening* André
Connors!

KONA WINDS *by Janet Dailey*
Happy in her teaching job in Hawaii, Julie then met her
pupil's grim half-brother ...

BOOMERANG BRIDE *by Margaret Pargeter*
Four years ago, when Vicki was expecting her husband Wade's
child, he had thrown her out. So why was he now forcing her
to return?

SAVAGE INTERLUDE *by Carole Mortimer*
James St Just was Kate's half-brother, but Damien Savage
didn't know that, and he had jumped to all the wrong
conclusions ...

THE JASMINE BRIDE *by Daphne Clair*
Rachel didn't think it mattered that she was so much
younger than Damon Curtis — but she was also very much
more inexperienced ...

CHAMPAGNE SPRING *by Margaret Rome*
The arrogant Marquis de la Roque thought the worst of
Chantal and her brother — but she was determined to prove
him wrong!

DEVIL ON HORSEBACK *by Elizabeth Graham*
Joanne went as housekeeper to Alex Harper — but he was
convinced that she was only yet another candidate for the
position of his wife ...

PRINCE OF DARKNESS *by Susanna Firth*
After five years' separation from her husband Elliott, Cassie
was just about getting over it when Elliott turned up again
— as her boss.

COUNTRY COUSIN *by Jacqueline Gilbert*
Eleanor liked the Mansel family. What a pity she couldn't
feel the same way about the son of the family, the uncompro-
mising Edward ...

Available December 1979

Forthcoming Classic Romances

THE TIME OF THE JACARANDA
by Margaret Way

The Australian station of Saranga boasted a beautiful old homestead, all colonial elegance of mellow sandstone and white cast-iron lace. Its owner, Grant Manning, was handsome, clever and a man to contend with. Adrienne saw the station as a means of escape — but how could she escape Grant?

THE SILVER SLAVE
by Violet Winspear

Rosary was confident that she was going to make a good job of tutoring a young Portuguese girl — but Gisela's father, the imposing Dom Duarte de Montqueiro Ardo, thought otherwise. Rosary was too young and inexperienced, he decreed. And that was not the only problem posed by Dom Duarte . . .

TANGLE IN SUNSHINE
by Rosalind Brett

Tessa had flown from England to Nigeria to attend her cousin Raine's wedding to Edward Grimshaw. Tessa liked Edward, so she was horrified to find on her arrival that Raine had transferred her attention to cacao expert David Clavering. Tessa instantly resented David on Edward's behalf; but as she grew to know him better, she found herself hoping on her own account that he might not be too deeply attracted to Raine.

LEGACY OF THE PAST
by Anne Mather

The only two men in Madeline's life so far had been gentle and kind, wanting only to protect and cherish her. Nicholas Vitale was anything but gentle, kind or protective — but Madeline couldn't resist him. But if she got involved with him, would she bring herself anything but heartbreak?

Mills & Boon Classic Romances
— all that's best in Romantic Reading

Available December 1979